HANNAH'S
COLORED PARADISE

A STORY OF SURVIVAL IN AMERICA

DURING THE TIMES OF

"SEPARATE BUT EQUAL"

1865-1965

Omer Ertur

OMER ERTUR

ISBN: 9798817565874

Published by Amazon Kindle Direct publishing, Columbia, South Carolina, USA

First Edition: June 2022

Revised Second Edition: June 2023

Omer Ertur: After acquiring a BA in Economics and an MA in Public Administration from Memphis State University, he received a Ph.D. in Urban Planning from Portland State University in Oregon. After a decade of teaching at the Iowa State University in Iowa, he joined the United Nations as a senior official. He worked in several countries in Asia and Africa as the Representative of various UN agencies. Since his retirement from the United Nations, he has published several books, mostly historical narratives, in four languages: English, Turkish, Japanese and Arabic.

ACKNOWLEDGEMENT

I dedicate this story to the memory of my brother-in-law, Dana Carlton Curtis Jr., a member of NAACP Memphis Tennessee Chapter, who worked hard for the establishment of the civil rights of African-Americans during the mid-1960s and to the memory of my Memphis Central High School homeroom teacher, Mary Elizabeth Smith, who taught me the basics of American history and the primary reasons behind the resurgence of white supremacy in America.

Omer Ertur
Ishigaki, Japan
June 14, 2023

HANNAH'S

COLORED PARADISE

OMER ERTUR

New Orleans 1856: Hannah for Fun and Pleasure

After counting the ship's African captives packed tightly in shackles below deck and checking each and every one of them for good health and proper appearance, the slave merchant walked up to the upper deck and handed the ship's captain a pouch full of bank notes and gold coins. Walking out of the slave ship *Clotilda* that had travelled from West Africa across the Atlantic Ocean and recently anchored at the port of New Orleans, Louisiana, the slave merchant ordered his assistants to remove the Africans out of the ship and transport them to the main slave market near the port facility.

At the slave market, arriving African captives were first assigned numbers for identification and then separated into gender and age groups. Following that process, several required legal forms were filled for each captive who would soon be sold and become a slave.

As this was going on, a tall and shapely adolescent African girl noticed her father at the far end of the large field, standing among a group of men in chains. She hollered to get his attention. When he turned his head and looked at her, she raised her arms high up in the air and with a forced smile on her face, she let him know she was all right by shouting, "I am fine, Father!"

She could not hear his reply. Trying hard not to cry, she waved her arms as she realized that she might not ever see him again.

After inspecting and assigning them into various sale categories and determining appropriate prices for all the African males, the slave merchant started his inspection of the females. He suddenly stopped in front of a tall, well-built, good looking young African girl with the number 14 hanging over her neck.

Intensely glancing at the half naked girl, he loudly growled, "This is an excellent merchandise. Let's put a high price on this one: say $900 and mark the sign as *'For Fun and Pleasure'*."

"What name should I assign her? How old do you think she is?" asked the assistant.

Still staring gleefully at the young African girl, the slave merchant promptly replied, "She looks like a Hannah to me! I think she is a thirteen-years-old young virgin chick."

Kangela, an adolescent girl from an Igbo speaking tribe living in Senegambia region of West

Africa, now renamed and registered as Hannah on the slave roster by a slave merchant, was one of the last African captives on an old copper-sheathed schooner named *Clotilda* that had arrived in 1856 in New Orleans, the North America's only remaining active slave trading port. These coffin shaped slave ships have been transporting millions of black African captives to Europe's and North America's ports since 1619. Regardless of the anti-slavery legislations enacted in many of the European countries since the end of 18th Century and also by the United State Federal Government laws that banned international slave trade at the beginning of 19th Century, the port of New Orleans had remained active to meet the demands of the North American slave markets and had continued to flourish until the beginning of the United States Civil War in 1861.

In time it became a well-known fact that nearly one-third of the kidnapped Africans perished on ships at sea due to unsafe and unhealthy seafaring circumstances and harsh treatments they had received from the slave-ship's personnel during the months long Atlantic Ocean crossings. Furthermore prior to boarding a slave ship for the deadly seafaring journey, many of the kidnapped African tribesmen, women and children died on their harsh and unsafe forced travels to the numerous slave port facilities along the West African shoreline.

CLOTILDA: LAST AMERICAN SLAVE SHIP

Upon arrival at a slave port facility, surviving kidnapped Africans were delivered to the slave-ships. After being separated into gender and various age groups, they were put in chains and forced tightly into the lower decks of the wooden sailing ships. Under such inhuman and unhealthy conditions, many of the African captives died and their corpses were thrown overboard to the sharks that followed the ships.

Upon reaching the Port of New Orleans, which was the slave-ship's final destination to disembark the cargo of surviving Africans, the captain of the ship, upon receiving a payment in cash, allowed the slave market representative to take over the valuable human cargo. This human cargo composed of kidnapped Africans, now owned by slave market operators, would soon be marketed at various slave distribution centers in New Orleans for further sale to various customers coming from wealthy entities with vested interests in commercial, agricultural and industrial estates that had prevailed in many parts of the American society of the time. At the slave markets, the representatives of these entities shopped for African captives to be used as household servants, farm hands and at times as factory workers.

The adolescent girl Kangela from West Africa, who was then and there renamed and registered as "Hannah" into the slave registry books, was now ready to be auctioned at the New Orleans slave market.

A few hours later, after being groomed and dressed in presentable clothes, Kangela was forced up to a sales platform. She now wore a large signpost around her neck that read 'HANNAH FOR FUN & PLEASURE'.

11

Later that afternoon, with an asking price of $900, she was sold for $600 to a New Orleans slave dealer, who was specialized in providing female slaves to the houses of ill-repute in and around the downtown New Orleans.

That same afternoon, Kangela and a few other female Africans were taken to the lobby of a major New Orleans hotel, where they were displayed for further sale to interested entities, mostly well-known prostitution houses in downtown.

A well-dressed madame of a bordello named *Paradise,* serving high-paying customers around New Orleans, bought Kangela for a hefty $800 and took the young African girl to her establishment located near the major hotels and businesses in busy downtown district.

Upon arriving at the house of pleasures, the madame ordered a middle-aged black servant to take good care of the newly purchased young African virgin named Hannah.

"She should rest at least for a few days. Make sure she is well fed. When she appears healthy and ready for action, let me know. Before offering her to our customers, we will dress her up in an attractive outfit and put some makeup on her face."

As she was walking out of the room, the madame was calculating in her head how much profit this good-looking black virgin would bring in after only a few tricks. As she closed the door behind her, she murmured, "I am glad I went to the slave market this morning. This was a very lucky catch indeed!"

A few days of rest and good food placed Kangela in relatively better physical health but her confused state of mind, full of anxiety and depression, became worse. She had no idea where she was, who these people were and what they wanted from her.

Staring out of the room's large window, she curiously watched the busy downtown street full of people and fast-running phaetons. She muttered to herself in Igbo, "I don't know where I am? This is a very different world, full of strangely dressed white people."

Turning her attention back to the room she was in, Kangela sat on the bed; closing her eyes, she tried to remember all that had happened during the past several months...

One warm, sunny morning, I was in the fields together with my parents. We were checking on the conditions of our cassava and sweet potato crops. A small group of men, wearing strange outfits and carrying rifles on their shoulders, suddenly appeared in

13

front of us. After tying our hands, they forced us to walk toward the nearby forest, where a large group of previously kidnapped villagers, mostly young adults, were gathered. Then they forced us walk for many days to the nearby seashore.

Upon reaching the shoreline, we were put on small boats and taken to a large wooden sailing ship. On the ship, mean-looking sailors separated men and women. After installing chains on our arms and legs, they forced us to move into the ship's lower deck. During the miserable, long night in that stinky, overcrowded area, I hung onto my mother's arms. The

next day early in the morning the ship sailed away. I had no idea where we were being taken.

A few days later, my mother became ill and fainted. She was caried away by two sailors. I tried talking to the women around me who spoke Igbo, but they had no idea where my mother was taken and what had happened to her. Standing up, I tried to locate my father. Far ahead toward the front end of the lower deck I could see him in chains among the male captives. He was too far away from me to get his attention. Later that horrible day, I was able to see him when we were taken to the upper deck for forced exercises. I shouted at him that mother was taken ill but I was all right. I am not sure he heard me. When I returned below deck, the woman chained next to me told me that one of the captive African boys helping the sailors above deck informed her that my mother had recovered from her illness in the ship's infirmary. When I asked her why she wasn't back here with us, she told me that the captain of the ship had decided to keep her in his cabin to enjoy her company.

A few days later, she told me that my mother the night before had jumped overboard into the dark sea and had been eaten by sharks that followed the ship. The next day, when I was taken up to the main deck for *forced exercises, as I pretended to exercise, I stared out at the sea and noticed a few sharks still following the ship. I started to cry and wondered why my mother killed herself...*

Opening her eyes in New Orleans, she realized that she was now in a strange room in a strange land. Tears running down her cheeks, she mumbled, "Why was I kidnapped from my village and brought to this faraway land?"

Suddenly, her caretaker entered the room and loudly asked, "How are you doing Miss Hannah?"

By now, able to recognize the slave-name she had been assigned, she hollered back in her native tongue, "Stop calling me Miss Hannah. My name is Kangela."

A few days later, the madame of the brothel decided that the young African girl Hannah was now ready to be displayed for business. The conniving madame was hoping for a rich customer who would be willing to pay a lot of money to have intercourse with a beautiful young African virgin.

In preparations to display her to prospective customers, Kangela was made to dress in a colorful cotton dress that showed her curvy futures. Then, the madame herself put makeup on her face and sprayed her body with perfumes to make her sexually desirable. During the early hours of the evening, she was taken to the well-lit entry hall to welcome the incoming customers. She and several other ladies of the night were lined up next to the wall, waiting for the arrival of men with deep pockets.

Kangela had no idea about what was happening around her. She stared at the girl next to her with a questioning look on her face. There was no reaction. Even if the girl next to her attempted to tell Kangela what was about to happen, highly confused African girl, who did not speak a word of English, would not understand a word of her explanation. Kangela cautiously moved away from the girls and went into a far corner of the room where she nervously and shyly watched the whole thing almost like a curious but scared spectator until one middle aged, short and chubby white man approached her and asked, "What's your name young lady?"

The madame who was nearby rushed toward the prospective customer and told him she was a virgin African girl named Hannah and told him what her price was. When the man made a counter offer, the madame refused the offer and told him if he wanted to have sex with a young virgin, that is what he would have to pay. After a few moments of indecision, the man, now smiling broadly, agreed to the asking price and paid the madame immediately in cash.

The customer was then ushered into a gaudy, sparsely furnished room with a large bed. He got undressed quickly. Sitting on the edge of the bed in his underwear, he impatiently waited for the young virgin African girl's entry.

The madame brought Kangela into the room. With a serious demeanor, she told the half-naked man to be gentle with her. Without waiting for his reply, she turned around and swiftly left the room.

At that point, Kangela finally had figured out what was about to happen. After the madame's departure, she quickly withdrew to the far corner of the room. The half-naked man slowly approached her with the intent to take her clothes off. Like a cornered cat, Kangela smacked the man on the groin with a tight fist. Then she hit him hard on the side of his face, knocking him flat on his back. As the man tried to pull himself up, Kangela kicked his head and ran out of the room. Before she could get near the main entrance door of the house, she was caught by the guards. The two heavyset, rough-looking men grabbed her and dragged her into the backyard. Throwing the young African girl on the ground, they started kicking her wildly.

Hearing the loud commotion, the madame rushed into the backyard. After shouting that they were damaging her property, she ordered the guards to stop. At that precise moment, Kangela's would be customer with a bloodied face came out to the backyard, carrying a long heavy metal rod with a serious intent to punish the African girl. The madame quickly got in front of the angry man and told him that she would give his money back plus another lady would be providing him with free services. Getting his money back, the man threw the metal rod on the ground and returned to the house.

Afterwards, Kangela was carried back to her room. Looking at her bloodied face, the madame asked her assistant to clean up her wounds.

The next day, realizing that the young African girl with a serious attitude problem would not be any use in this kind of business, the madame ordered her assistant to take Kangela back to the main slave market to be resold.

The following day, Kangela was put back on the sale roster of the auction block with several other black women with identification tags that read "GOOD FOR HOUSE SERVICE AND FARMWORK".

As she was pushed again on the slave sale platform with several African women, Kangela took a look at the tag that was placed around her neck. She recognized her recently assigned slave-name 'Hannah' but could not understand the rest of the sentence that read, "*Experienced Household Servant and Strong Farm Hand*". Given her past family farming experience at her African village, most of the sentence, unknown to Kangela, were basically true.

That day in early February 1856, Kangela, as identified on her slave records as 'Hannah', was purchased by a slave merchant from Natchez, Mississippi, a small port-city on the Grand Old River. Her new owner would take Kangela and all other newly purchased slaves to Natchez, located around 400 miles north of New Orleans, to be resold to many slave-masters that came regularly from the large cotton plantations nearby.

The next day, all of the recently purchased slaves and many large crates containing various farm supplies were placed unto a big steam-propelled barge to travel north toward the port of Natchez on the Mississippi River. All of the slaves sat shoulder-to-shoulder on the wet floor, leaning against large wooden crates that were securely placed in the middle of the deck.

As the loaded, slow-moving barge traveled against the river's strong current, Kangela, wondering where she was being taken to, curiously watched the everchanging landscape and the scraggy shoreline full of overgrown vegetation fed by the muddy waters of the Grand Old River. When the barge passed several settlements near the shoreline, Kangela raised her head high to glance at the town's people sullenly walking around the pedestrian walkways.

Twice a day, two armed guards served the slaves large, over-cooked cathead corn biscuits and drinking water in metal cups. If any slave needed to respond to nature's call, there was a large bucket at the backend of the barge to be used in the open. When the bucket was full, the last slave using it would empty the bucket into muddy waters of the river.

As she sat apprehensively on the bucket in front of other slaves and several guards, Kangela thought, *"This is a little better than the situation I faced on that horrible slave ship that brought me to this strange land."*

On the slave ship, she recalled, *"I had to call the guard to unshackle me, allowing me to reach the bucket that was in the middle of the lower deck. Sitting on the bucket, I was surrounded by a large crowd of chained slaves. Worst of all, when I requested to access the bucket, many times I was completely ignored by the guards. I would then defecate on the floor I was sitting on. I was not the only one who ended up doing that; many slaves who were tightly confined in chained positions in this stinky, foul-aired place had to relieve themselves on the floor. By the late afternoon, as we sat in our own excretes, we had to breath the stinky foul air until the next morning's forced exercise session that would remove all of us up to the main deck. During our forced exercise sessions, ship's crew would wash the soiled floors below deck with buckets of sea water."*

•••

After two nights of stopovers at local port facilities, the barge traveling on the Mississippi River reached the Port of Natchez late afternoon of the third day. The slaves were taken out to a grassy open field and placed in a large canvass tent. The next morning, with their identification tags around their necks, one by one they were again put on a high platform to be sold.

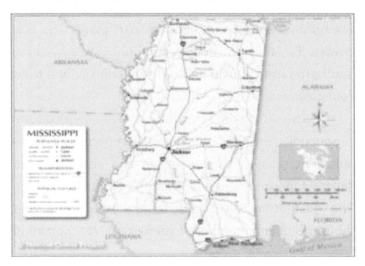

A few days later, Kangela and two young male African slaves were bought by a white slave-master of a large cotton plantation located near the Mississippi River town of Greenville, right across from the state of Arkansas.

At the Mississippi Cotton Plantation

After nearly all-day ride on a long and wide four horse-drawn wooden cart, loaded with large bags of farm supplies and three African slaves in shackles, entered through the main gate of a 3000-acre cotton plantation located nearly twenty miles of north of the town of Greenville and 150 miles south of the city of Memphis, Tennessee. This immense plantation was owned for nearly three generations by a wealthy southern family: David and Dorothy Franklin and their four children.

The Franklin plantation, an agricultural production entity, considered economically self-sufficient, grew cotton for profit and also produced several types of grains and vegetables for consumption. The plantation also had many fruit trees and maintained large number of animals for transportation use.

The plantation had ninety black slaves, one third of which were females, who were mostly used in the common kitchen facility and in the plantation mansion's household services such as cleaning, cooking, washing and ironing.

Most of the male and a few of the female slaves, under the guidance of a white slave-master named Steve and his two assistants, efficiently but at times rudely managed the slaves working in the cotton fields and, in the meantime, guided the wheat and oats planting and maintained various vegetable gardens and fruit trees. They also took care of farm animals such as horses, donkeys and mules and managed the care and slaughter of cows, pigs and chickens that were raised in the plantation.

In 1856, the State of Mississippi, like most of the southern and a few of the northern states, legally allowed slavery to remain a part of the local economic framework. Slaves were treated as property with practically no rights or freedoms. They were bought and sold in various slave markets all over the state. If any of the slaves misbehaved, acted disrespectfully or did not work hard enough, the punishment would be anything from a heavy scolding to a bloody whipping. If they escaped, they would be pursued by slave-catchers and law enforcement officers. When caught, they were severely punished by the slavers with whippings and imprisonment.

...

Stepping off of the horse-cart in front of a large wooden storage shack, where carts and phaetons were kept, Kangela, standing erect, intensely browsed her immediate environment. Everything that surrounded her appeared strangely different than what she was used to seeing around her father's farm in West Africa. In her village, her family lived in a large thatched-roof hut that was surrounded by numerous chicken coups and large cultivated fields of sweet potatoes and cassava.

Now in this new landscape, she glanced intensely at the tall trees, plush greenery and vegetation that surrounded her. She realized that she was in an entirely different world. Also, looking at the buildings around her, she noticed how different and colossal these wooden and brick structures appeared compared to the thatched-roof huts she lived in her African village.

As she sullenly stood in front of the wooden cart, she suddenly remembered again all that had happened since she was kidnapped from her village. She recalled the scarry, dark faces of the African kidnappers who were clad in black, strange-looking outfits and spoke a tongue she did not understand. On the big wooden boat, the sulky, bearded faces of mean-looking white sailors, carrying long wooden sticks in their hands, were permanently etched in her memory. Everyone on that miserable ship looked, dressed and talked so differently and acted so violently that she could not make any sense of what was going on. The only thing she was able to grasp that she was being forcefully taken to a very far away land. Not yet aware of the reasons behind her forced relocation, Kangela felt completely lost. All these traumatic and sorrowful memories suddenly made her extremely sad; feeling dizzy, she crouched on the ground.

Steve, the slave-master, approached her and ordered her to stand up and follow him. When Kangela did not respond, he grabbed her arm and forced her to stand. He then dragged her by her arm to a large wooden building that was the plantation's kitchen facility located near the two-floor white plastered large colonial style mansion of the plantation owner.

Entering the immense food preparation facility that fed nearly one hundred people three times a day, Steve brought Kangela in front of an overweight middle-aged black woman and released her arm.

Glancing at the plantation's senior cook with an obvious sneer on his face, he said, "Mama Rose! Here's the kitchen help you've been asking for."

Looking intensely at the young slave woman, Mama Rose inquired, "What's your name, girl?"

When there was no reply, Steve, looking at the papers in his hand, replied, "The document says her name is Hannah. I leave her in your good hands Mama. I got to hand these papers to Master David."

After Steve's departure, Mama Rose summoned a kitchen helper nearby and asked the black woman to take the newcomer to the slave quarters behind the kitchen facility. She ordered her to show the new slave girl her bed, assist her to take a bath and give her a clean set of underwear and a uniform to wear.

"Before we eat our meals this evening, bring her to the dining area. Tomorrow morning, I'll decide what kinda work she gonna do in kitchen."

This was the beginning of Kangela's new life as a slave in a cotton plantation in Greenville, Mississippi. During the next few months, she eventually grew to accept her slave-name Hannah. Also, during that time she fully grasped the full meaning of being a slave. After making some mistakes, she realized that to survive as a slave she had to accept her fate and do properly and efficiently what was expected of her. She became a quick learner as she carefully followed Mama Rose's daily instructions.

After a year working in the kitchen, she learned enough English to express herself and be understood. During that year, she focused on learning the basics of cooking and baking. But mostly she learned how to properly use the huge cast iron stoves and the large, heavy cooking pans and utensils.

During that time, Hannah's unfailing hard work in the kitchen did not go unnoticed. Mama Rose immensely appreciated her and one Sunday morning, she decided to take Hannah together with the kitchen crew to the church services in the town of Greenville, twenty miles south of the plantation.

After a long horse-buggy ride to the First Baptist Church in Greenville, Mama Rose and the kitchen crew entered the church building and climbed the stairs to reach the upper balcony, the only place in the building where slaves were allowed to gather and pray.

Hannah was amazed with the immense and colorful interior of the church. She immediately went to the front section of the balcony and looked down at the church's main floor full of well-dressed white families in their Sunday garments getting ready for the Sunday prayers.

Upon returning to her seat, Hannah wondered about the reason why she was brought to this building. She had many questions in her mind about the purpose of such a gathering but because of her limited English, she remained silent.

At the end of the Sunday morning prayer service, as she walked out of the building, she stopped in front of a black preacher, who also happened to be the conductor of the choir.

Looking at the preacher, Hannah asked, "What's Holy Spirit?"

Pointing at the book he was holding tightly, the black preacher calmly replied, "Young lady, you can find the answer in the Bible."

"But, sir!" Hannah hurriedly responded, "I no read!"

"What's your name girl and which plantation you come from?"

After whispering her name, Hannah raised her hand to point at Mama Rose standing nearby.

The preacher, recognizing Mama Rose, turned around and called to a young girl standing among the group of black choir singers to come closer.

"Miss Hannah, this is Nancy. She knows how to read and write. She also lives in your plantation. If you meet her during the evening hours and Sundays, she's gonna teach you reading and writing."

Thereafter, Nancy and Hannah would meet regularly in the late evening hours at a quiet corner of the immense kitchen facility. This is how Hannah learned how to read and write.

Soon Hannah and Nancy became good friends; actually, good enough for Nancy to become the protective big sister of Hannah. After many evenings at the back of the kitchen facility, Hannah's grasp of English language became good enough for her to have actual conversations with Nancy.

One hot summer day, Hannah was asked to bring some fresh supplies from the vast vegetable garden where Nancy worked. On her way to the vegetable garden along the plantation's wide main road, she noticed two male slaves in chains being dragged by two uniformed policemen on horses. On reaching the garden, she told Nancy what she had seen.

Nancy sullenly responded, "Three days ago them slave boys escaped from plantation. Police grabbed them foolish boys before they got to Memphis."

"What's gonna happen to them boys now?" asked Hannah.

"They gonna be severely whipped and gonna be locked in a shack for long time. If they escape again, they gonna be put away for good."

"If them boys got to Memphis, they gonna become free, right?"

"No, that ain't correct! They ain't gonna be free by reaching Memphis. Folks against slavery in Memphis gonna hide them boys and then help them escape to north where slavery ain't allowed."

Not able to fully grasp the meaning behind what Nancy had told her about folks against slavery, Hannah stopped asking questions.

That evening, when Nancy came to the kitchen for Hannah's reading lessons, she told her more about the two escapees.

"This afternoon, in front of cotton-field workers, them two boys got beaten badly by slave master Steve's two helpers. Two bloodied boys was thrown into a shack. Them boys gonna remain there for long time."

Hannah was sad hearing about what had happened to the escapees. To change the subject, Hannah asked Nancy, "Tell me how you learn reading and writing?"

"I got me a good teacher." replied Nancy. "I was born here and raised on plantation. A free black man named Joe, a carpenter from Greenville, came to our plantation for woodwork and repairing wooden things, you know, tables, chairs, cabinets and wardrobes. During Joe's work visits, my parents ask him to our shack for supper. One evening Joe asked me if I could read. I told him I ain't learn reading. He then ask how old I was. Learning I was seven years old, he ask my parents why no one teach me reading. My father told Joe us slaves ain't allowed reading and writing. I guess, Joe, a free black man, didn't know us slaves ain't got no permit reading. Seeing a bible on corner table, Joe asked why we got a book in the house if no one gonna be reading it. My mama told him she got Bible while visiting church. Joe then ask my papa's permission to teach mama and me reading. That's when we began our reading lessons. Thanks to that nice man, three years later, my mama and I read whole Bible."

"Joe still coming to the plantation for woodwork?" asked Hannah.

"He ain't coming here no more. He got ill and died a short while ago. Ned, his son, now run Joe's carpentry shop in Greenville."

"You told me you share your shack with a young man named George. I guess you ain't living with you parents no more. Where are them now?"

"My mother died two years ago. After her death, my father gone very sad; he stopped working. So, slave-master Steve ain't happy with him not working, so he take him to Natchez slave market and sell him last year.

I think now, my father live in plantation south of Natchez."

"I understand, you now gonna live with George. One day ain't you gonna have George's baby?"

"No, I ain't gonna have his baby. To do that, first we gotta have plantation master's permission to marry and then his agreement for us to have a baby. Worst of all, the baby gonna become Master David's property."

"I don't understand. Why your baby gonna belong to Master David?"

"Because us slaves belong to owner. When born, a slave baby also gonna become owned by him."

Even though this conversation did not help Hannah grasp fully what had been revealed by Nancy, she came to a much broader understanding of the true meaning of being a slave: a person without any rights, freedoms or privileges.

Nearly two years after Hannah's arrival at the plantation, one late evening Nancy waited in the back of the kitchen for a long time for Hannah's arrival. When she did not show up, Nancy decided to check on her. She went to the slaves' living quarters behind the kitchen. Entering the large room full of beds, Nancy saw slave-master Steve arguing in a highly aggressive manner with Hannah in the secluded far corner of the room.

Noticing Nancy's presence, Steve hurriedly left the room.

Running toward Hannah, Nancy quickly asked, "He's after you, ain't he?"

"I think so. He tried to take off my clothes."

"That's how he raped me years ago. Ain't you lucky I came here looking for you. You be sure girl, you never alone in this room."

"What I do now, Nancy?"

"There ain't nothing you can do. If you fight him, he'll punish you real bad."

As they walked back to the kitchen, Hannah told Nancy about her bad experience in a New Orleans whorehouse. Hearing the story, Nancy told Hannah that she was lucky to survive such an ugly ordeal. Then, sitting around the old wooden table, they started their daily reading and writing exercises.

Suddenly, closing the Bible she was reading, Hannah said, "I got an idea. You gonna get me a pen and writing paper?"

"I gonna get them for you but you tell me why?"

"I wanna write a letter to big boss. I'm gonna tell him about what happened this evening."

"If you do that Steve surely gonna punish you bad. You gonna be beaten and taken off kitchen duty and taken to fields to pick cotton."

"Maybe so! But maybe Master David gonna have talk with Steve so he gonna stop chasing after me."

Shaking her head, Nancy said, "That's you wishing girl! Writing to Master David ain't gonna do nothing like that. You be wasting your time."

"Please Nancy, get me paper and pen. Ain't you gonna do that for me?"

"Alright, I gonna get them for you."

The next evening, after receiving a pen and a clean sheet of paper, Hannah spent a long time composing a letter to Master David. She had seen the big boss once leaving the plantation on his fancy phaeton and twice talking to Head Mistress Mary. He appeared to her to be in his early forties and seemed to be a man with kind disposition.

After introducing herself in the letter by clearly stating her name and age. Then she simply asked the owner of the plantation to protect her from the unwanted advances of Master Steve.

That evening, when a few servants from the mansion arrived at the kitchen to take some prepared dishes to be served to the owner's household, Hannah asked one of the servants to give her letter to Master David. The servant nervously agreed to deliver the letter but later decided not to hand it directly to the Master. Many days later, as she cleaned Master David's study, she left Hannah's letter on his desk.

During that time, the slave-master Steve took Hannah away from the kitchen and reassigned her to the cotton fields work team. After a few days of torturous work at the vast open fields from sunrise to sundown, Hannah, became exhausted and disenchanted. Now heavily depressed about Master David's decision to punish her for the letter she had written, she staired at her dirty, swollen hands and began to cry.

She did not know that her letter had not yet reached the eyes of the Master. Assuming that Steve would try to rape her at the first opportunity, she whispered, "I now knows why my mama jumped into sea to die."

She carefully placed a small rusted knife that she found in the cottonfield into her side pocket and murmured with a hateful glare in her eyes, "If Master Steve put hands on me again, I'm gonna cut his throat."

The next morning, Master David discovered Hannah's letter on his desk. After reading it, he took the letter to the breakfast room and shared it with his wife.

Reading the letter, Mistress Dorothy turned crimson red and abruptly asked her husband, "I hope you're going to do something about this letter?"

The same afternoon, Hannah was brought back to her kitchen duties. A day later, Mistress Dorothy unexpectedly visited the kitchen and had a long talk with Mama Rose about Hannah. Learning that she learned how to read and write since her arrival at the plantation nearly two years earlier, Mistress Dorothy decided to use Hannah in her house. Early in the evening, she was transferred to the servants' quarters in the plantation's mansion.

Hannah, now working as a house servant in the plantation master's mansion, was overwhelmed with the size of the large residence with two immense floors. Every one of its sixteen rooms and four bathrooms were full of heavyset furniture and numerous decorative items.

As she carefully dusted the furniture, she looked around and muttered to herself, "They got things and more things they ain't gonna use. I wants to know why so many us slaves only help six of them. My whole village in Africa gonna live in this big house."

During the coming year Hannah learned practically everything about housework, including cleaning, ironing, setting tables and many other house maintenance assignments that were given her by the house headmistress named Mary, who managed the group of fifteen slaves that took care of the owner's family of six.

One day as she was cleaning Master David's study, Hannah noticed a library case full of leather-bound books. Ever since she learned how to read, she was constantly reading and re-reading the Bible that was given her a long time ago by the black preacher. Suddenly realizing that the Bible was the only book she ever read, she wanted to read a new book. So, the next day she asked the Headmistress Mary if it was possible for her to borrow one of the books from the master's library. Mistress Mary told her that she would ask the master.

A few days later, the master's oldest son Michael brought a few books from his own library and handed them to Hannah. He then asked Hannah to return the books to his room when she finished reading them. A month later, she returned the books she finished reading. She was then allowed to borrow a few more books to read.

It took Hannah a bit longer to finish reading the last group of books she borrowed because it was the cotton-picking time in the plantation, which lasted nearly a month. During that time of the year, most of the servants in the mansion and the kitchen were asked to join the field workers to gather all the puffy white cotton flowers. They first had to pull the cotton balls from the stems and stuff them into the small bags on their shoulders. They would then empty the small bags into large containers. When full, these large containers were taken to a building where the cotton was ginned.

After returning to her household duties at the main mansion, Hannah was able to finish reading the last book she had borrowed: Robinson Crusoe. When she took the book back to Michael's room, she saw a tall, good-looking young black man building a library case on the far end of the large room.

Noticing Hannah entering the room, the young man stopped working and turned toward her. With a warm, bright smile on his handsome, slender face, he introduced himself, "My name is Ned Blum. You must be Hannah. Nancy told me all about you. I'm glad to meet you, Hannah."

Hannah, now also wearing a sincere smile on her face, shyly replied, "I'm glad meet you, Ned."

She then placed the book in her hand on the table and walked out of the room.

As she resumed her cleaning duties at the mansion's main floor, she was excitedly thinking about the handsome young man she just met in Michael's room.

...

After the completion of Sunday church service in Greenville, Nancy invited Hannah to her humble shack near the vast vegetable garden. Back at the plantation, they found Nancy's boyfriend George sleeping on an old lounge chair in front of Nancy's shack.

George had never joined Nancy for the Sunday church services. In the recent past, when Nancy had asked George to join her, George had nonchalantly replied, "It's hard enough for me to provide free labor for my rich white master who gonna get more rich. I ain't gonna pretend to believe in his God."

Nancy and Hannah quietly pulled a couple of old wooden stools out of the shack and sat near George. Waking up, he smiled and started a conversation about certain rumors he had heard about the upcoming conflicts between slaver states and states which did not support slavery.

He curiously asked, "You girls heard anything about such hearsay at church meeting?"

Nancy replied, "No, we ain't heard no such thing."

As they kept on talking about other matters of the day, feeling hungry, George asked Nancy to get some baked goods from Mama Rose's kitchen. Before Nancy could depart for the kitchen, Hannah noticed the arrival of a small single-horse drawn phaeton slowly approaching them. Recognizing Ned, Hannah stood up and gently walked toward the phaeton to welcome him. When she reached him, Ned was about to remove a musical instrument from the back of the phaeton. Hannah greeted him warmly with a broad smile.

Smiling back, Ned said, "It is nice to see you again Miss Hannah."

As they walked back to the shack, Nancy, noticing the guitar in Ned's hand, excitedly hollered,

"Ain't we lucky today! We gonna hear Ned sing us wonderful songs."

Nancy then rushed to the kitchen facility to get some food. A few minutes later she came back with a basket full of baked goods including Mama Rose's famous pecan pie.

As they gobbled down Mama Rose's delicious delicacies, Ned played his guitar and sang some of his own melodic sad blues. Nancy, who was also a good singer, joined him sing with harmony in some of the songs she knew.

That afternoon, Ned and Hannah took a long walk on the plantation's wide promenade lined with tall acacia trees. As they walked with happy smiles on their faces Hannah said, "You sing very good Ned. How you learn to play that music instrument?"

"It's a long story Hannah, but I'm gonna tell you all about it. Several years ago, my father and I went to Memphis. A friend of my father had just moved to a black neighborhood of Memphis. He invited us to help him build an eatery. As we were building the eatery and the necessary furniture for my father's friend, I visited a few of the nearby pubs in the evenings. In one pub, I listened to wonderful songs sung by black performers and saw a guitar first time in my life. One evening my father joined me to visit a pub with two black musicians performing. As they strummed their guitars, they sang beautiful melodic songs that were called blues."

Interrupting Ned, Hannah asked, "Blue colored songs? I don't understand."

"In our slave language being blue means feeling sad. Blues are sentimental songs about the sufferings of us slave folks."

Hannah excitedly interrupted Ned, "Aint that a fact. When I think about my village in Africa, I'm gonna be blue. Is that so?"

Smiling, Ned replied, "Yes, that is exactly how you would feel. Now let me continue with my story. Hearing those sad songs played wonderfully on such musical instrument called guitar, the next morning I told my father that I would like to learn how to play guitar. Same evening, we visited the same pub for my father to listen blues songs. When the musical performance ended, my father went to the stage and asked the musicians their permission to have a close look at one of their guitars. A few months later, in our carpentry shop in Greenville he made me a guitar. I had to wait for many months for strings to be brought to Greenville by a friend coming from Memphis."

"Ain't that a wonderful story! I wanna know how you learn playing that instrument named guitar?"

"I taught myself!"

"But then ain't you learn them wonderful songs from somebody."

"Most of the songs I sang today are my own. I composed them. But I also learned some other songs from a few musician friends."

As they walked, they talked in more detail about his compositions of sad but melodic songs revealing dramatic stories about captivity and forced displacement of natives of Africa and their endless suffering as slaves. Ned explained to Hannah that the songs were mostly about being homesick and missing loved ones.

Stopping and looking at Hannah affectionately, he said, "Blues songs are about immense inner sufferings inflicted upon the enslaved African natives living in America."

"Ned, but you ain't a slave. Nancy says you is a free black man."

When Hannah uttered those words, she was not aware that a free black man was not truly free; he could only retain his free status if and when a white man would agree to be his personal guarantor.

Ned cautiously replied, "That's true, I'm a free black man. Being a free black man is just another kind of slavery. As a free black man, I don't have the basic rights given to white men. I'm not truly a free person because I'm not allowed to move away from here without my white guardian's agreement. I can't get married to a white woman or a slave woman. I could only marry a second-generation free black woman."

"Tell me what's a second-generation free black woman?" Hannah inquired.

"A woman born into already freed black parents."

"If she a free black woman, then she gonna be allowed marrying a slave man?"

"Sometimes, in some states a free black woman might be allowed to purchase a slave man, but she would not be allowed to marry him. You see, by marrying him she must to be considered the head of the household. Like with white families, the rule is that the man is always the head of the household. Because of this, a free black woman can't marry a slave man."

Not fully comprehending the meaning behind Ned's complicated explanation, Hannah commented, "I got your meaning, you only a little better than us slaves. Tell me the name of your last sad song."

"*Winds of Freedom*!"

Misunderstanding what she heard, Hannah responded, "Wings of Freedom! Beautiful song!"

Smiling broadly, Ned corrected her: "Not wings but winds of freedom. But, you know, I think I like your version 'Wings of Freedom' much better. From now on that song will be called by that title."

As they resumed walking, Ned said, "Nancy told me that you're learning to read. Tell me what made you be interested in reading?"

"When I got to church first time, I asked preacher question. He gave me his Bible telling me answer gonna be in God's book. Then he told Nancy teach me reading."

"By now, you must have finished reading the Bible. Are you interested in reading other books?"

"There ain't no books in kitchen to read. I now in master's house. I borrow books from young master. Ned, you read many books? You got schooling, ain't you? I guess you is, because you speak like them white folks."

"My father, who taught Nancy to read also thought me to read and write. I also attended Sunday school classes at the church to improve my English. I have a room full of books in my house. I've already finished reading most of them. You're correct; more I read more I speak like the white folks. If you keep on reading, in time you'll also speak like white folks as well."

Then, as Ned talked about some of his favorite books in his library, Hannah secretly glanced at his handsome face, thinking, *"I like him. I'm gonna fall in love with this man."*

This was the beginning of a happy courtship period between Hannah, a slave working as a maid at the Franklin Plantation mansion, and Ned, a freed black man, who earned his living by doing carpentry work in many plantations around Greenville, Mississippi.

Six months later, following the celebration of the new year 1860, Ned asked Hannah to take a walk with him on the riverfront promenade after the Sunday church services in Greenville. Outside the church, Hannah approached Mama Rose and asked for her permission to let her have a few hours with Ned.

Mama Rose, shaking her side to side, responded negatively.

"Horse-buggy soon gonna depart for plantation. I ain't gonna leave you behind, how you gonna get home, girl?"

49

Before Hannah could respond, Ned replied, "Mama Rose, please don't worry. I'll bring her home in two hours' time."

A few minutes later, as they walked side by side on the riverfront promenade lined with tall and wide oak trees near the First Baptist Church, Ned asked Hannah to become his partner for life.

Hannah, stopped and turned around; wearing a broad, happy smile on her face, she swiftly replied, "Your question got me very happy, Ned. Yes, I'm gonna be your…" She could not complete the sentence.

Ned finished it for her, "Partner for life."

Unfortunately, what Ned asked could not have been a proper marriage proposal, because, in most of the southern states a slave woman would not be allowed to marry a free black man.

The only thing Ned could do was to purchase Hannah from the plantation's owner. Even if Master David agreed to sell Hannah to Ned, that would only make Hannah a property of Ned, plus they had to acquire an agreement from Ned's white male guarantor for Hannah's sale to Ned to take place. Even if they were somehow able to do that, they would not be allowed to marry in the state of Mississippi, nor in any other southern state that allowed slavery to exist.

...

A few months later, Ned was asked to come to the Franklin plantation to fix the leaky roof of the mansion. As he prepared to get on the roof together with George, Ned asked Mistress Mary to arrange for him a meeting with Master David. Later that afternoon, he was directed to go to Master David's study.

Upon entering Master's study, Ned noticed that Master David was busy reading a document on his desk. Ned, hesitating, quietly waited at the doorway.

Master David, noticing him, raised his head abruptly and said, "if you have a question about the roof repair, you should ask Steve."

Ned replied, "Sir, I want to talk to you about a personal matter."

Without any expression on his face, Master David asked Ned to take the seat in front of his desk.

Sitting uneasily in the leather armchair, Ned nervously told him about his personal relationship with one of the slave servants working in the mansion.

Master David abruptly asked, "Who is she?"

"Her name is Hannah!"

"Hannah... Yes, I remember her. She is a smart and hard-working girl. Isn't she a bit too young for you?"

"I think she is almost eighteen years old, Sir."

"What is your intension?"

"We want to become a family, Sir."

"Are you aware that as a free black man you cannot marry a slave?"

"I am well aware of that, Sir. I came here to ask you to allow me to purchase her from you. I have enough savings to pay you whatever she's worth. If you agree to release her, we'll have a life together."

After remaining silent for a short while, Master David finally replied, "I have to think about your proposal. Mistress Mary will soon tell you my final decision."

Ned, feeling nervous and frustrated, stood up and walked out of the study. He had hoped a more positive reaction from Master David.

When he got back on the roof, he told George about the meeting with Master David.

"I think it was wishful thinking on my part. I don't think Master David will ever sell her to me. I don't know what I'll do now?"

George calmly replied, "There ain't nothing you can do, Ned."

As they continued to work on the roof, George told Ned about the news he heard about the formation of a regiment of colored army troops in some of the northern states. He declared that one day he will escape and join the Union Army's colored regiment.

A week later, the roof work was completed. Mistress Mary, as she paid Ned for his work, she told him Master David's reply. As Ned correctly expected, Master David did not want to sell Hannah to Ned.

Reacting to Master David's negative reply, Ned decided to escape with Hannah to Memphis. He discussed that possibility with Nancy and George; they were strongly against it. They reminded him that if they get caught, state authorities would jail both of them for a long time. They suggested Ned should try again to purchase Hannah from Master David.

Ned, rejecting their suggestion, replied, "Talking to Master David again would not produce any positive result. I'm sure he'll not change his mind. He doesn't give a damn about us black folks. When it is the right time, Hanna and I'll escape to Memphis."

By late autumn of 1860, after discussing with Hannah the full details of his plan and receiving her agreement, Ned started to prepare for their escape to Memphis. He shopped for a stronger and larger buggy that would be pulled by two horses. At one of the plantations he worked, he found a big old horse-drawn carriage in relatively good shape. He bought it and took it to his workshop in Greenville.

He immediately started to work on the old carriage to convert it to run with two horses. During the early part of the spring of 1861, he purchased one more horse. After hooking both horses to the refurbished carriage, he took it out for a trial on the dirt-roads around Greenville.

During the last week of March, he packed all of his carpentry tools into the back of the carriage and safely placed his guitar, a few bags full of clothing, several personal items and a few of his favorite books over the well-packed tools.

The coming week, he sold his house and the carpentry shop to an interested white family for cash payment with a stipulation that he would remain in his house for a short while until he was ready to relocate.

The Civil War and the Emancipation of Slaves

At the end of the first week of April 1861, various rumors about the possibility of several southern States' breaking away from the Federal Union were circulating in and around many of the Mississippi plantations. During the same time, David Franklin, a former US Army cavalry officer, received a written order asking him to report as soon as possible to the Confederate Military Headquarters in Montgomery, Alabama to serve as a cavalry colonel. He appropriately informed his wife Dorothy about his decision to join the Confederate Army.

The American Civil War began on April 12, 1861 in South Carolina by a Confederate Army attack on the Union held Fort *Sumpter* in Charleston Harbor. After the commencement of the civil war, the Confederate Forces focused their attention to occupy Federal

Union's capital Washington, while the Union Forces prepared plans to attack the Confederate State of Tennessee.

Following the formation of a separate confederation by thirteen southern states, a full-blown, bloody military conflict ensued on the border areas identified as the Mason Dixon demarcation line between the northern and southern states. Both armies attacked each other viciously at various border areas. At first, both sides claimed victory after almost every battle. But soon it appeared that the Union Army was slowly gaining the upper hand in the ongoing conflict.

•••

One sunny late April morning, soon after the beginning of the civil war, David Franklin, wearing a dark grey Confederate colonel's uniform, got on his horse and departed from the plantation. Before departing, he told his wife Dorothy that the Confederate Army would definitely win the coming civil war and he would soon return home.

Obviously, the Colonel Franklin was wrong; he incorrectly had assumed that the Confederate States would be victorious and the civil war would end within a short period of time. The civil war between the states would last nearly four years and cost the lives of seven hundred thousand men.

Following Master David's departure from the plantation and immediately after the completion of the Sunday church service, Ned took Hannah, Nancy and George in his rebuilt carriage back to the plantation. Sitting in front of Nancy's shack, they discussed the news about the ongoing civil war that would soon spread all over the country.

This was the crucially important news Ned was waiting for. He kept thinking that during the absence of the plantation's master and mostly due to ongoing intense military conflicts, he and Hannah might be able to safely escape to Memphis without being apprehended by the law enforcement. He again revealed his escape plan to Nancy and George. This time, both of them firmly nodded their heads indicating their full agreement with his plan.

Ned then loudly declared, "Next Sunday after church services, Hannah and I will definitely leave Greenville for Memphis."

Looking at Nancy, he continued, "Please make sure after our departure, Hannah's absence would not be noticed by anyone in the plantation for a while, at least until the next morning."

Immediately after the conclusion of the following Sunday's church service, Ned and Hannah said their farewells to Nancy and George in front of the Baptist Church in Greenville. As he shook Ned's hand, George wished them a safe journey and whispered that he soon would also escape from the plantation and join the colored troops of the Union Army. Hugging Nancy, Ned reminded her to do her best to hide Hannah's disappearance from the plantation as long as possible.

After the sad and teary-eyed farewells, Ned and Hannah quietly walked away from the church grounds. They reached the fully loaded two horse-drawn carriage hidden behind thick bushes and tall trees near the river. Hannah brought with her only a small bag containing a few personal items: a pair of clean underwear, a comb and a toothbrush. As he helped Hannah into the carriage, Ned told her to take off her slave uniform and change into the new set of ladies' clothes folded neatly on the seat. He then warned her to keep the carriage's curtains closed at all times.

Before closing the carriage's door, he looked at her lovingly.

"My darling Hannah, I am now at your service as your personal coachman. From now on until we reach Memphis, I'll do everything possible for us safely reach our destination. Before sunset, we will find a safe place to spend the night in the carriage. If you get hungry or thirsty, in the basket next to your feet there are some food items and a bottle of drinking water."

As she settled into the carriage's cushioned seat, Hannah smiled happily and said, "Hey you coachman! You gonna be nice to them horses. Don't you be so rough with them."

Climbing onto the driver's seat, Ned replied, "Yes, madam. I'll treat them gently."

After saying a few prayers for a safe journey, he smacked the horses rear with a whip. Holding the reins tightly, he guided the carriage into the nearby dirt road.

As the carriage sullenly moved on the road, Hannah, now comfortably settled inside the coach, tried to relax. The time up to their departure from Greenville was full of so many events that Hanna was not able to come to terms with her feelings about their escape from the plantation. For the first time in her life, she doing something she wanted to do. Suddenly horrors of being caught by law enforcement entered her mind. Remembering how badly the captured slaves were treated by the police, she closed her eyes, full of fear of being caught, she started to pray. But then she remembered Ned's words that due to ongoing conflict they would safely reach Memphis. Now full of elation and anticipation of a happy life with the man she loved she opened her eyes. Now, she was sure of one thing: she was happy about her decision to start a new life with Ned.

During their first day of travel, Ned, purposefully rode the horse buggy slowly to give an appearance of a leisurely journey. An hour before the sunset, he noticed a small wooded patch of land near the river. Parking the carriage in front of a set of tall bushes right next to a grassy green pasture, he helped Hannah to get off the carriage. He unhitched the horses and tied them to a tree with a long rope allowing them to feed. Then, together with Hannah, he placed a large cotton sheet over the grassy ground and emptied the basket containing food and a bottle of drinking water.

As she prepared their supper, Hannah inquired, "How many more days we gonna travel to Memphis?"

"Hannah, please remember, we are in the middle of a civil war. We have to travel cautiously in disguise; most people seeing a carriage with a black coachman would assume it's carrying white folks. If we're lucky, we'll not run into military convoys and police officers. If we ride nonstop directly to Memphis, it would have taken us only one full day to reach the city. However, because we are travelling slowly, it might take us a bit longer."

As they were calmly enjoying their early evening meal before sunset, Ned reached into his side pocket and took out a gold ring that had been worn by his deceased mother. He softly held Hannah's left hand and gently placed the ring onto her finger.

Looking at her lovingly, he whispered, "My beautiful friend Hannah, would you become my wife and spend the rest of your life with me?"

Staring at the shiny gold ring on her finger, Hannah murmured, "Of course, Ned. I want nothing more. I'm very happy to be your wife."

Intensely staring at the ring on her finger, she asked, Such a beautiful ring! Where you get it?"

"It was my mother's wedding ring. Now it belongs to you."

"I wanna know more about your mother."

"She was a Chickasaw princess, the eldest daughter of a tribal chief. A few years after my father's death, she became ill and passed away."

"Chickasaw! What is them?" asked Hannah.

"The original inhabitants of the lands surrounding Mississippi River before the white people arrived. The Chickasaw Tribe was kicked out of the State of Mississippi by the Federal Government before I was born. They now live on a faraway land somewhere in the mid-west region of the country."

"How your father meet your mother?" asked Hannah.

"It's getting dark. We have to get back into the carriage and prepare for the night. I'll tell you all about my parents tomorrow."

The next day, they traveled nonstop toward Memphis. Before sunset, finding a secluded wooded area, Ned parked the carriage and fed the horses. As he prepared a bucket of water for the horses, he told Hannah that they were very close to Memphis but for safety reasons they would enter the city the following morning after dawn.

Eating their evening meal surrounded by large oak trees, Hannah commented that she now realized why Ned appeared so different and handsome.

"I knows now you is different because you is half Negro and half Chickasaw."

She then asked Ned to continue with his parent's story.

"Like you, my father was also kidnapped from a village in West Africa as a young man and brought to America on a slave ship. At the Natchez slave market, he was bought by a Jewish furniture builder from Greenville, Mississippi."

Suddenly realizing that Hannah may not know anything about Jewish people, he briefly explained that the Jews were a group of white people worshiping a different God. Then realizing his mistake, he said, "No, that is not correct. They believe in the same God but they just pray differently."

After that brief explanation, he continued, "A carpenter named Simon Blum bought my father. When Simon was a young child, his family migrated to America from a European country called Prussia. After purchasing my father, Simon named him Joseph and trained him to become a good carpenter like him. He also taught my father how to read and write. Within a few years, my father had become a reliable carpentry assistant to this good-natured man who was also an excellent furniture maker. After his wife's unexpected sudden death, Simon, who had no children, decided to free my father. After, signing the necessary papers that

64

made my father a free black man, he told him that he was now free to go wherever he wanted to live the rest of his life. When my father became a free negro, he chose to take Simon's last name Blum and informed him, because of his kind decision to set him free, he would remain with him as a salaried carpenter. My father told Simon that his shop and home were the only things he valued in his life. A few years later, before passing away, this kind Jewish man made the necessary legal arrangements to leave the carpentry shop and his house to my father."

"Such a good man!" said Hannah. "You gonna tell me now how your father meet your mother."

"One day when my father was working in his shop, one of his white customers stopped by to visit him. He was a merchant selling goods to Chickasaw and Choctaw Indian tribes living around Greenville. He asked my father if he would build a raised wooden bed for the Chickasaw tribal chief Tishomingo to use in his tepee. A few days later, my father, loading his tool box on a mule-drawn cart, took a long ride to the tribal area. After reaching there, he agreed to barter a few tribal items such as wood blocks and dried animal skins for his services. He then built a solid wood raised-bed frame in tribal chief's teepee for the old warrior to sleep on. During that time my father met one of the old chief's daughters named Lushanya, meaning 'songbird' in Chickasaw language. My father learned that a few years earlier Lushanya's husband had been shot and killed by a group of white farmers. So, after they became interested in each other, together they approached her father, the chief of the tribe, for his permission allowing them to marry. My maternal grandfather, whom I never had a chance to meet, agreed to my father's proposal to let Lushanya, his eldest daughter, to become the wife of this successful and free negro carpenter. Soon after my mother's arrival at our home in Greenville, the Chickasaw tribe was forced out of the state of Mississippi by the Federal authorities. A few years later I was born."

Hannah asked, "Ain't you speaking any Chickasaw language?"

"Not so well, but I can utter a few basic sentences."

They kept talking about Ned's family for many hours. After sunset, when it was almost completely dark outside, they swiftly moved into the carriage to spend the night. Snuggling tightly to each other, they were soon asleep.

Life on Beale Street

The next morning soon after dawn, they entered Memphis on a rough dirt road along the river. Soon, they reached the black neighborhood surrounding Beale Street.

At the beginning of the civil war the city of Memphis had a population of over twenty thousand people, one fifth of which was composed of colored folks most of whom were the former slaves or the recent escapees who lived in the densely packed Beale

Street neighborhood located at the south eastern end of the city near the fast-flowing Grand Old Mississippi River.

Ned easily found the eatery that he and his father built a few years earlier. When Hanna and Ned entered the eatery that was located on the crowded part of Beale Street, the owners Robert and Hazel, recognizing Ned, warmly welcomed him. After meeting Hannah and hearing about her escape from a plantation in Greenville, Robert told Ned that they were welcome to move into the old wooden shack behind the eatery. After moving their belongings into the shack, Ned hid the carriage behind some bushes in the backyard. The following day, he sold both horses in a nearby market.

Under generous and caring attention of Robert and Hazel, Ned and Hannah's settlement into a new life around Beale Street commenced comfortably and securely. A few days later, Hannah, started working discreetly in the rear section of the eatery's kitchen where she was not exposed to any customers. Soon, with Robert's guidance, Ned also found a parttime job repairing old furniture to earn additional income. He also joined a group of musicians performing at a nearby Beale Street pub during the weekend nights.

Though they were comfortable in the old shack behind the eatery, Ned told Hannah that they would rent a better place to live in as soon as it was safe for her to be seen in public.

"Actually," he continued calmly, "when the civil war ends, we might purchase a big old house and build a carpentry workshop on the property with the money I got from the sale of my shop and the house in Greenville."

Looking at him lovingly, Hannah told him that as long as they were happy and healthy, everything would work out fine. She then suddenly remembering something that had been bothering her for a long time, she asked, "Tell me why white folks gonna keep on killing each other to free us slaves?"

"I don't think they are killing each other just to free slaves. I think there is more to it." replied Ned. "There might be many more hidden reasons behind such a bloody conflict. But whatever those reasons are, for our sake, I hope Northern states will be victorious at the end."

"I hope so too!" replied Hannah. She then quickly inquired, "I remember you telling me you brought your books with us to Memphis. Where is them books?"

Ned immediately went out to the carriage hidden behind the eatery and brought back a small box full of his favorite books. Hannah excitedly checked the box and selected two books to start reading: *The Lewis and Clark Expedition* and *The Life of Frederick Douglas*.

During the rest of the year, Hannah and Ned happily survived in that little old shack waiting for the civil war to end. They were seriously concerned that under a Confederate Army victory, as escapees they would be severely punished and would possibly become slaves again. They prayed for a Union Army victory but, by any chance, if the Confederate Forces were victorious, they considered escaping from Memphis to California where the former slaves were welcomed.

By the beginning of the summer of 1862, the Northern Union Army, already in eastern Tennessee and the Union Naval Forces successfully operating on the Mississippi River, fully occupied the confederate State of Tennessee and pushed the Southern Confederate Army out of Memphis across the grand old river into the Confederate states of Mississippi and Arkansas.

After a year of living in Memphis with constant concerns of being apprehended, Ned and Hannah welcomed the arrival of the Union Army into Memphis with great joy. When the Union soldiers set foot in Memphis, Ned and Hannah, feeling that they were finally fully liberated, joined the crowd of celebrating former slaves on Beale Street.

Now feeling safe and secure, Hannah suddenly felt free to do the things she loved doing during her early adolescence at her village in Africa. She loved taking long walks in the pastures surrounding her village. So, following the arrival of the Federal Army to Memphis, on several afternoons she took long walks on the dirt road along the river near Beale Street.

During some of the long walks, she sometimes fearlessly took a detour and ventured into the narrow back streets of the black neighborhoods. As she briskly walked through densely built shacks that were shabbily constructed from discarded pieces of wood planks, used bricks, broken cement slabs and old metal pieces, she noticed several well-dressed young women wearing heavy makeup casually strolling around the shabby neighborhood streets.

71

Not understanding what was going on, upon returning home she asked Ned about it. Ned nonchalantly told her that those girls were waiting for customers.

Arms crossed and eye brows raised, Hannah immediately inquired, "What them girls gonna sell?"

Ned with an inquisitive look on his face replied, "With your horrible experience in the New Orleans whorehouse, you should be able to figure it out. These girls are out on the streets to sell the only thing they have, their bodies!"

Hannah, irritated with Ned's reply, responded quickly, "I ain't wanna remember them horrible New Orleans days but thinking about them days in New Orleans gonna make me wonder what's gonna happen them jobless girls. I got another question for you, Ned. What's gonna happen with them young men? Since nobody wanna pay for their bodies, what they'll gonna do?"

Pointing at the latest Memphis' Daily Commercial Appeal newspaper on the workbench, Ned replied, "To survive, they would just steal whatever they can. This article in yesterday's paper says that many slaves from the nearby states have escaped to

Memphis. Most of the newcomers have no jobs, and they become either thieves or prostitutes."

Ned then read Hannah the rest of the newspaper article.

"Before the arrival of the Federal Union Army, nearly twenty thousand people lived in Memphis, one fifth of which were blacks. After the arrival of the Union forces, many white families moved to the nearby Confederate states of Mississippi, Arkansas and Louisiana. In the same time, many slaves from the southern plantations escaped to Memphis. As a result, nearly one third of Memphis' total population of thirty thousand are now composed of black men and women living in densely populated shabby unkept neighborhoods."

The following Sunday morning, Hannah suggested to Ned that they visit the nearby black church. That would be their first church attendance since their escape from Greenville. Entering the First Baptist Church in the black neighborhood, Hannah noticed that everybody attending the service were black, not a single white person was present in the building.

The Sunday service was conducted by a black Baptist preacher and followed by several spiritual songs performed by an all-black neighborhood choir. Realizing that the most of the spiritual songs performed by the choir were based on the well-known traditional Negro folk songs, Ned was impressed with their performance and decided to join the choir.

After the Sunday church service, Hannah and Ned took a walk along the riverside road. As they walked calmly on the well-packed dirt road that followed the fast-flowing river, Ned softly murmured, "I already told you all about my family. Why don't you tell me about your family now?"

Hannah abruptly stopped walking and turned toward Ned.

"Every time I think about my life back in Africa, it hurt me head so much I wanna cry. So, I ain't gonna tell you now. I promise, one day, I'm gonna surely tell you all about my village in Africa."

The following day, hearing about the establishment of new rules and regulations by the Northern Union Army that would protect former slaves, Ned decided that it was the appropriate time to buy a house in the sprawling black neighborhood surrounding Beale Street. Soon after discussing his decision with Hannah and getting her agreement, he bought a big old colonial style wooden house with a huge front porch. Soon after purchasing it, he converted the back part of the house into a carpentry workshop. He then rebuilt the front section of the house as a spacious, comfortable living area. In this newly established carpentry workshop, he labored very hard to make furniture for sale. At the same time, he also started to perform regularly at a Beale Street pub during the weekend evenings to earn extra money.

Hannah was very happy to move out of the old shack and settle into a spacious house full of handsome wood furniture pieces made by Ned. While keeping a very comfortable and spotless home to enjoy her day-to-day life with her partner Ned, she continued work in the eatery.

A few months later, Ned started performing at various local pubs almost every evening. One night after completing his performance, Ned was approached by a young white man, who profusely congratulated him for an outstanding stage performance. Introducing himself, he told Ned he was a former Union Army officer from Pennsylvania. He then informed Ned that he just had started a house construction company in Memphis. When Ned informed him that in addition to being a singer, he also was a carpenter, the man from Pennsylvania asked Ned to help him with his ongoing residential building projects in various white neighborhoods of Memphis.

Soon after being fully involved with the construction projects in the white neighborhoods as a carpenter, Ned hired two young former slaves to help him with the heavy lumber work. During the process of hiring the two young former slaves to help him, he realized the degree of desolate poverty among the colored folks living in his neighborhood. He noticed that most of the newly arrived former slaves had poor health, practically no incomes and lived in desolate housing conditions.

Discussing the matter with Hannah, he declared, "These former slaves live in the most miserable of circumstances: they got no money, not enough food and no proper shelter over their heads."

"But now at least them is free to make good life for themself." replied Hannah.

"That is true if they had some education but most of them can't read or write and don't have any skills to find work to make money. Without any basic of skills, how could they start a new life as a free negro?

How can they find jobs to survive? At least as slaves, they had shelter over their heads and some food in their bellies. Under the new federal rules applied in former confederate areas freed by the Northern Army, many former slaves had no choice but remain in plantations. They could become contractual workers, earning very little money but paying their former master for rent and food. I say, that is another form of slavery. So, no one should blame the contracted negroes escaping from plantations. If we can find a way to help the new escapees to learn reading and writing and acquire some basic skills, then they might find jobs and become truly free."

Hannah, looking at Ned, said, "You is correct! You started helping them two boys by employing them in your wood working project? You gonna train them become good carpenters like you is. I think, we gonna talk to preacher coming Sunday. He's gonna let us teach them former slaves reading'n writing after church service?"

"That is an excellent idea, Hannah. Let's do that."

Following this discussion, that is exactly what they did: They started a small reading and writing class for some of the illiterate former slaves that had recently joined the church. Hannah also started a small reading class for the former slaves working in the back of the eatery's kitchen as dishwashers and cleaners. Furthermore, Ned held a carpentry training session in his workshop for several willing former slaves living in their poor neighborhood.

One day in early 1865, Ned purchased a horse and brought home his old carriage that had been hidden for couple of years in the backyard of the eatery. He cleaned it thoroughly and made it ready to run. One sunny Sunday afternoon Hannah joined him for a joyful sightseeing ride on the riverside dirt road.

A few days later, hearing that the Union Army successfully occupied most of the State of Mississippi all the way down to Natchez Port on the Mississippi river, Hannah asked Ned, "You think we gonna send a letter to Nancy?"

Ned replied, "Let's go to the post office and find out."

That afternoon they rode their carriage to the main post office at the city center to get an answer to Hannah's question. They were informed that it was now possible to send mail to some parts of Mississippi, including Greenville. The next day Hannah wrote a long letter to Nancy and asked Ned to mail it.

Almost three months later she received a reply from Nancy. In her letter, Nancy informed Hannah that George had recently escaped from the plantation and joined the Federal Union's colored regiment. She also wrote that Master David had been severely wounded in a cavalry battle and was now recovering at a South Carolina military hospital. She ended her letter with a statement that she constantly prayed the Lord to end this bloody Civil War with a definite Federal Army victory.

...

With the surrender of Confederate Armed Forces in the State of Virginia on April 9, 1865, the Civil War had ended with a complete victory for the Federal Union Forces. Nearly seven hundred thousand Federal Union and Confederate soldiers had perished in the four-year conflict. Immediately after the end of the war, the Emancipation Proclamation, the presidential executive order that had already been issued in early 1863, was immediately put into action by President Lincoln immediately freeing all the slaves in the former Confederate States.

The following day, there were joyful celebrations on the streets of negro neighborhoods of Memphis. Almost all of the residents in neighborhoods

79

surrounding Beale Street, many of whom were former slaves that had escaped from various southern states, excitedly danced and chanted loudly on the streets to celebrate the beginning of their new lives as free people.

One late Saturday evening, not long after the arrival of Nancy's letter, Ned was performing with his band at a Beale Street pub. A tall black sergeant wearing a dark blue union army uniform entered the pub and waived at Ned performing on the stage. With a broad smile on his face, he shouted, "I knew I find you here."

The sergeant then took a seat near the stage to listen Ned sing.

Completing his last song, Ned, stepped off the stage and approached George. As he gave him a bear hug, Ned told George that he looked good in Union Army uniform. For almost an hour, as they drank several glasses of beer, they talked about many things, mostly about their personal experiences since their escape from the Greenville plantation. Ned asked George many questions about the day-to-day life of colored folks in the military service. George told Ned that they were constantly training for possible field action.

"After I became a sergeant," George explained, "I became responsible for the mess tent operations. You know that gave me access to extra food."

Ned, smiling, responded, "I noticed that you look strong but a bit heavy. Have you been to the frontlines' fighting?"

"No, most of us ain't asked to go frontlines. Only a small well-trained group of chosen colored soldiers, commanded by white officers, asked to go to front to fight the Confederate Army. So, I now hear them colored soldiers courageously fought the enemy."

Completing his sentence, George finished his beer and stood up. "I gotta get back to base. I like to see you and Hannah soon. I got a day off in two Saturdays from now."

"We'll pick you up at noon with my old carriage. Where's your base?"

"Just go north on the riverfront dirt road until you see military barracks on your right. I'm gonna be waiting at main gate at noon. See you then!"

Returning home that evening, Ned wanted to tell Hannah about George's unexpected visit but he did not want to wake her up. Early the next morning, as Hannah was preparing to leave the house for work, Ned told her about George's visit and that in two weeks they would visit him at the military base in North Memphis.

The same afternoon, finishing her kitchen duties at the eatery, Hannah rushed home. Entering Ned's workshop, without saying a word, she stood in front of him with tears rolling down on her cheeks. Ned, stopping what he was doing, asked her what was wrong. Hannah hurriedly told him that President Lincoln had been assassinated.

Ned, hearing that horrible news, now in shock, silently stood in front of the bench. Then he walked toward the solid wood couch and sat down. Hannah snuggled next to him; as they bowed their heads down, they whispered prayers. After remaining silent on the couch for a long time, they walked out of the workshop with sad and sulky faces. At the front porch, they sat shoulder to shoulder on the wide wooden steps and talked about what would be the future impact of the assassination of the man who made it possible for the slaves to be free.

With a gloomy face, Ned whispered, "Lincoln was a great leader. It is unfortunate that they got him killed hardly a few days after the war's ending. I don't think southern white people will never let us be free.

They will keep on fighting to keep us colored folks down in the gutter."

"It's gonna turn out that way; ain't it? Who now become the new president?" asked Hannah.

"Andrew Johnson, Lincoln's vice president, will be sworn in as the new president."

"New president gonna change government's intention to free slaves?"

"I don't know, Hannah. We will soon see what happens?"

Nearly two weeks later, Ned and Hannah got into their carriage and started their short journey to the military base to meet George. As they were traveling on the riverside road, they suddenly came upon a large number of people crowding the riverfront road. Glancing toward the river, Ned noticed a large number of uniformed corpses were floating on its surface. They were being plucked out of the water by many Union soldiers in small boats.

Leaving the carriage, Ned walked to the riverfront and asked someone in the crowd what was going on. He was informed that the steamboat named *Sultana,* carrying a large number of Union soldiers and

Confederate prisoners, suddenly and unexpectedly exploded, killing thousands of people on board.

Returning to the carriage, he told Hannah what he had heard.

She asked, "Why steamboat explode?"

"Nobody knows. It may be the result of a sabotage, or maybe it was just an accident."

Hannah, staring at the Grand Old River full of floating corpses, sadly remarked, "This bloody war never gonna end, ain't it?"

As he nudged the horse to move the carriage forward, Ned sullenly replied, "You got it right, it might never end!"

That afternoon they had a great time with Sergeant George as their guest. At Hannah and Ned's home, they enjoyed a delicious supper of barbecued pork ribs, fried potatoes, corn-on the cob and blackeye-peas. During the supper, George informed Hannah that Nancy might soon arrive in Memphis on a river boat coming from Greenville. Hannah, excited about the news, told George that Nancy is welcome to stay with them.

A couple of months later, during one late sunny afternoon, Nancy, carrying a small bag, appeared in front of Hannah's door steps. Hannah welcomed her friend with a warm hug. That day, Ned was away building a house in a white neighborhood, so the two friends talked for hours and hours. Nancy told Hannah that immediately after the war had ended, several Union officers arrived at the plantation and forced Master David to free all the slaves.

Hannah, excited about the news, declared. "I wish I was there... Tell me more."

"Master David told the union officers letting them slaves free is gonna be very bad for plantation because it now is crop-harvesting time. Union officer told Master David he must let slaves free and give them contract who wanna remain at plantation. Officer then told Master he gonna pay them money for work. This exactly what happened. Most of us colored folks ain't got no option but to remain in plantation and sign them lousy low-paying contract. You know almost all them colored folks in plantation ain't reading. So, they just put X on them contract without ain't knowing what's gonna happen. I didn't want to stay in that damn plantation, so I told them I ain't signing no contract and left the plantation soon afterward. Here I am. By the way, when we gonna see George?"

"I think we gonna take you to military base tomorrow and let him see you. Soon George get himself a furlough, he's gonna come here to be with you. Now I'm gonna show you your room."

As planned, early in the afternoon of the next day they went to the Union Army Colored Regiment Base. George was very happy to see Nancy. As they kissed and hugged each other passionately, Hannah whispered to Ned, "Ain't them two is crazy about each other. I bet you, they gonna get married soon."

Before they departed from the base, George told them that the following Saturday, he will get an overnight furlough.

The next morning Hannah took Nancy to the eatery to introduce her to the owner's wife Hazel. That afternoon Nancy started to work in the eatery as a parttime dishwasher. A few weeks later, she joined Hannah in the main kitchen and became a fulltime cook's assistant.

A month later, with her own income and George's military salary combined, Nancy was able to afford to rent a small old house nearby Hannah and Ned's residence. From then on, George was able to get frequent weekend furloughs to stay in his new residence he shared with Nancy. Not long after that, Nancy joined Hannah and Ned as a teacher in their literacy classes at First Baptist Church. She also joined Ned in the church's choir.

Memphis Race Riots of 1866

In early May 1866, on a warm Saturday evening, George and a few of his colored soldier friends in full army uniforms arrived at the pub where Ned's trio was performing. During the later part of the evening, two of George's friends, now heavily intoxicated, walked out of the pub for some fresh air. Outside, they were confronted by two white Memphis policemen. Seeing the uniformed policemen in front of them, both colored servicemen straightened themselves and stopped giggling.

One of the white policemen, facing the colored soldiers, shouted, "You stupid boys, what do you think you're doing?"

"We ain't doing nothing Sir! We just wanna have good time."

"No, you don't boy! You're just behaving like goddamn niggers. You're both are under arrest."

Refusing to accept the insulting words uttered by the aggressive white policeman, one of the colored servicemen quickly punched him to the ground. When the other policeman reached for his gun, the other colored soldier quickly approached him, grabbed him and not allowed him to take his gun out. While this was going on, George and three other uniformed colored soldiers came out of the pub to help their two friends. Being surrounded by six black uniformed soldiers, the two policemen ran away to their nearby police station to get some help.

As far as the colored soldiers were concerned that was the end of the confrontation with the police. Realizing what might happen next, Ned turned toward George and hastily told him that that many policemen might soon come back to arrest them. He suggested that he and his friends go to Nancy's house and hide there for the night. So, George and his friends spent the night at Nancy's house. The rest of the night was uneventful; no police force came back to the Beale Street pub looking for the colored soldiers.

The next day early in the morning, Ned took George and his friends to the army base in his carriage. When he was almost back home, Ned noticed at the entry to the black neighborhood a large crowd of armed white men. The threatening mob, led by many policemen, was slowly approaching Beale Street.

Deciding quickly to avoid the crowd, he used the back streets to reach home. Getting home, he moved the carriage into the backyard and put the horse in the large shed. He went into the house and informed Hannah about the armed crowd moving toward Beale Street.

"What are we gonna do now?" Hannah nervously asked.

"We should hide in the shed." replied Ned and then he grabbed his shotgun and went out to the backyard.

A few minutes later, Hannah, carrying a few valuable personal items in her arms, came into the shed and noticed the loaded shotgun in Ned's hand.

She hollered, "Where did you get them rifle?"

"I bought it from Robert. He has many guns at the eatery, so he sold me one."

"You know how you gonna use it?"

"Yes, I do. When I was a boy, I used to go hunting with my father."

As Ned was watching through the opening of the shed door, suddenly, out of nowhere Nancy rushed into the backyard, screaming, "White people with guns gonna kill us all. Them attacking us coloreds on the street and setting them houses on fire. They threw them torches burning my house down. Now, I come here to tell you."

Ned told Hannah and Nancy to hide behind the shed. Getting his shotgun ready, he joined them.

SCENE IN MEMPHIS, TENNESSEE, DURING THE RIOT—BURNING A FREEDMEN'S SCHOOL-HOUSE.
[Sketched by A. E. W.]

Hardly a few minutes later, a large crowd appeared in front of the house and threw burning torches at their front porch.

After the violent crowd moved away to the next street, Ned, Hannah and Nancy rushed to the house and worked hard to put out the ongoing fire that was spreading out of control. The front part of the house, where they lived, was completely burned down but luckily Ned's work shop at the back of the house had very little damage. For the time being, unfortunately, Hannah and Ned had no place to live in but the work shop.

As Hannah and Ned were cleaning up the mess, Nancy ran back to her house and came back quickly with the news that her house had been completely destroyed. So, she also joined Ned and Hannah to live in Ned's workshop for the time being.

During the following three days, the armed racist mob, led by the police force, killed forty-six black men, raped many black women and burned down many houses and several black community buildings including all three black churches and six black public schools.

As the uprising was going on, the Union Army and the Memphis police force did nothing to stop the murderous and violent outburst of racist attacks by the racist members of the white community.

Though, a few months later, the Memphis race riots were investigated by the Federal authorities. However, nobody from the white community of Memphis and not a single officer from the Memphis

Police Force was criminally charged for the racist and violent acts they committed against a striving black community. Furthermore, nobody in the black community was ever compensated for his or her financial loss.

The only positive governmental action that came out of the horrible Memphis race riots in May 1866 was the adoption of the 14th Amendment by the United States Congress that allowed the former slaves to be recognized as United States citizens. However, despite the constitutional effort that recognized the citizenship of the newly freed slaves, the 14th Amendment did not result in bestowing the freed slaves with their basic civil and voting rights. On the contrary, in time it further inflamed the white communities' rejection of the equal civil rights of the former slaves, resulting in numerous violent reactions that would soon destroy many successful black settlements that came into existence in various urban areas since the end of the civil war.

As a result of three days of rioting in Memphis, which was led by the local police, most of the pubs where Ned performed, many black establishments, as well as many houses, including a part of Ned's house and the house that Nancy and George rented, were burned down. The eatery where Hannah and Nancy worked was also partially destroyed. After repairing the front part of his house, Ned, together with George, helped the owners Robert and Hazel to rebuild the eatery. After a few weeks of work effort, the eatery reopened its doors to customers and soon both Hannah and Nancy were back to work.

A few days later, Ned returned home after informing the white owner of the building contraction firm that he was no longer interested in building white folks' houses. He then told Hannah about his wish to leave Memphis.

Speaking softly yet with conviction, Hannah reacted, "It ain't a bad idea we gonna move away from Memphis. But why you think we gonna have a better life in the next place we live?"

"I don't have a proper answer to your question but I'm now sure about one thing: Memphis is not the place where we should spend the rest of our lives."

It took Ned and Hannah more than a year to prepare to leave Memphis, Tennessee. After completely renovating his heavily damaged house, he sold it at a loss to a conniving black real estate man, who was on his way to becoming the richest black man in Memphis.

Ned made some repairs on his carriage and bought two new horses. He packed all of his tools and placed all their personal items into various parts in the carriage's storage area and adjusted the back seat leaving enough space for Hannah to sit comfortably. They were now ready move away from Memphis.

One early fall day in 1867, after bidding goodbye to their friends Robert and Hazel at the eatery and visiting Nancy and George in their new rented house, they got into their well packed carriage and left Memphis for good to settle in a fast-growing black neighborhood in a faraway small town named Wilmington in the State of North Carolina.

Soon after their carriage reached the outskirts of Memphis, Hannah sticking her head out of the carriage's window curiously asked, "Ned, tell me why Wilmington?"

"I heard good things about that town from Robert. He told me that one of his friends moved to Wilmington before the civil war. At the end of the war, he wrote to Robert that living in that small black neighborhood during the civil war had been safe and prosperous. I think, we're going to have a great new beginning in Wilmington."

As they rode out eastward from Memphis on a county dirt road, they passed through Shelby Forest. Staring intensely at the magnificent tall trees and the beauty of nature surrounding them, Hannah remarked, "This is a gorgeous forest, I'm gonna be sorry that we leave Memphis for good. How long it's gonna take us to reach where we're going?"

"We have to ride completely through two states: Tennessee and North Carolina. If all goes well, we'll reach the town of Wilmington on the Atlantic Ocean's shoreline in about ten days' time."

"Ain't North Carolina a former confederate state?" asked Hannah.

"Yes, it was. But Robert's friend wrote that even during the war, Wilmington's white community treated the black residents fairly well. The new President, Andrew Johnson, is from North Carolina. I expect he'll make sure under the newly established federal regulations the former slaves will have more opportunities to improve their lives."

Before leaving Memphis, Ned had stored piles of dry feed for the horses on top of the carriage and a large container of water at the back of the storage area. Every evening, after finding a secure location to spend the night and safely parking the carriage, he fed and watered the horses. He then set up a bonfire while Hannah prepared the evening supper and the following morning's breakfast. On the road, they would basically survive on dried beef and biscuits.

On the third day of their trip, they reached eastern Tennessee. Before the sunset, Ned noticed a few black workers on a large tobacco field. Approaching one of the workers, Ned asked him where he might get some animal feed. The man told him that at the east end of the next town named Pulaski, he would find a shop that sells animal feed. Ned thanked him and while turning around, he heard the worker add under his breath, "Maybe sir you best not go there."

Ned promptly asked him why. The colored farmworker firmly replied, "Them white folks in Pulaski ain't like us negroes. In many occasions, them whites dress up in white hooded attires and ride their horses in the dark hours of the night to scare us colored folks. Few weeks ago, a group of them white folks, calling themselves KKK, lynched a negro boy for talking to a white girl. So, I suggest you look for an animal feed shop at the next town."

Ned decided not to enter the town of Pulaski and let the horses feed on fresh grass on the field where they spent the night.

After six more uneventful days, they reached the border of North Carolina. Soon after entering the state, they passed through many scenic valleys, plush green forests, deep blue lakes and fast flowing white water rivers. Amazed at the natural beauty of North Carolina, Ned stopped the carriage several times to enjoy the grand scenery.

Three days later, they finally arrived at the outskirts of Wilmington, a beautiful port city located on the coastal area of Cape Fear facing the Atlantic Ocean.

Wilmington, North Carolina

After finding the black neighborhood at the northwestern edge of the port city, Ned asked a few people on the street the location of a lumberyard owned by Philip, a friend of Robert and Hazel.

Finding the lumberyard in his new hometown was a very special occasion for a very capable carpenter like Ned. Philip, a middle age, short and stocky colored man, welcomed them warmly. After they exchanged some pleasantries, Philip told Ned that he could use one of the half empty storage shacks in the lumberyard to live in until he finds a place to rent.

Philip's wife Dollie came out to meet them. She was a tall, thin, and light-brown skinned woman with a broad smile who hit off with Hannah right away. Dollie took Hannah to the kitchen in their home in the back of the lumberyard where two ladies together prepared lunch.

During the lunch, Philip told Ned and Hannah they did the right thing by moving to Wilmington.

"The State of North Carolina and the town of Wilmington will become a place of good fortune and prosperity for the colored folks who work hard. Here in Wilmington, we are allowed to build our own community and take care of our own needs. Here we run our own schools, operate our local healthcare facilities and hopefully soon we'll open our own local banks. I expect that very soon we'll have here in Wilmington a large colored community that is independently operating and self-sufficient."

Ned asked excitedly, "Would the white community allow that to happen?"

"Yes, they will allow. The leaders of the white community in Wilmington always emphasized that a thriving and developing colored neighborhood would be good for the whole community, including the folks in the white neighborhoods."

Looking sullen, Ned replied, "Unfortunately, this did not happen in Memphis. The white community there decidedly destroyed a viable colored community because they could not stand their former slaves becoming successful businessmen. I think you're right! We did the right thing by deciding to move here."

Shortly after arriving at Wilmington, with the help of Philip, Ned, with the cash he brought from Memphis, bought a large house and established a carpentry workshop near the center of Wilmington's black neighborhood. Soon after that, he built a furniture display room next to the carpentry shop. Within a short period of time, his efforts started to bear fruit. With the earnings from his carpentry shop, he bought a small house in a busy part of the downtown near the business center of the black neighborhood of Wilmington for Hannah to establish a barbeque chicken eatery.

During the coming two decades, Ned and Hannah realized that they finally found the colored paradise they were searching for. The black neighborhood of Wilmington was growing so rapidly that soon it became a fully functioning economic entity with its own schools, healthcare facilities and banks that were fully managed by black professionals. Ned and Hannah finally registered their marriage legally in 1868. Two years later they had a daughter and named her after Hannah's mother *Zahara*, meaning *'flower'* in Igbo language.

In time, due to their hard work, Ned and Hannah Blum became a relatively wealthy black family because Ned's a carpentry workshop and a furniture store was doing very well and Hannah's barbeque chicken eatery in downtown of the colored neighborhood also became a successful business.

Now feeling confident about the future of his fast-developing community, Ned bought a big old house nearby Hannah's eatery in the black neighborhood and rebuilt it as a beautiful, comfortable home for the family. After completing the reconstruction of the old house, Ned finally joined a small blues band. He performed during the weekends at various local pubs that were frequented not only by colored but also the white folks of Wilmington.

One spring afternoon in 1872, as they enjoyed a beautiful sunny day in their well landscaped backyard garden, Hannah and Ned shared a few recent memories of beautiful times they had in their recent past since their escape from the cotton plantation.

Watching their daughter play on the grass, Ned glanced lovingly at Hannah.

"You know, our daughter will become a beautiful lady like you."

"She's gonna resemble my mother. I think, she's gonna become a gorgeous woman like her."

"I am sure of it. Like her namesake, she'll become a true flower of beauty. By the way, what is your father's name?"

"His name's Jawara, meaning a lover of peace. I know it ain't no more possible for us find my father but I wonder where he is. You think, he's still alive?"

"Let's be hopeful and imagine that he started a new family during his time as a slave and now he possibly lives with his new family somewhere in the deep South. I like his name very much. If we have a son, let's name him after your father."

That afternoon, Hanna finally told Ned about her parents and her life as a child in the West African village. When she was telling Ned about how she and her parents were kidnapped and forced into a slave ship, she started to cry. Pulling herself together, she managed to continue telling Ned about the horrible ocean voyage that brought her to New Orleans. After a short break, she also told him again about the horrible time she had in the whorehouse.

Affectionately looking at Ned, she completed her life story, "I was sold again in New Orleans and brought to Mississippi plantation, where I meet you my love."

A few years later, Hannah became pregnant again. To their disappointment, she had a miscarriage at the late stage of her pregnancy. When the nurse, helping Hannah recover from miscarriage, told her that the unfortunate unborn infant was a boy, Hannah decided not to mention it to Ned.

Regardless of the miscarriage, Ned and Hannah were very happy indeed in their colored paradise. The city of Wilmington was growing fast, its population had doubled since Hannah and Ned's arrival. Many new black businesses had been established and many black professionals had moved to Wilmington. The city now had a black owned law office, black dentists, doctors and most importantly several black policemen.

However, as many things had improved in this burgeoning black neighborhood of Wilmington, many negative political changes were about to occur in the state North Carolina, making the future prospects of the colored community of Wilmington not so promising.

At the end of the Civil War, as a former confederate state, North Carolina was allowed a special re-entry into the Federal Union under a Federal Government appointed Governor, William Holden, who immediately held a convention to determine the future of the rogue state. The convention abolished slavery, ratified the 13th Amendment and abolished all debt resulting from the Civil War.

This new beginning for the former confederate state enabled its economy a full recovery. Resultantly, many former slaves had moved into North Carolina as agricultural workers and town dwellers.

In time, the political power structure of the state fell under the control of northern liberal intellectuals, who were referred by the former confederate politicians as the carpetbaggers. Arriving northern intellectuals, in cooperation with the local white liberals, who were crudely called as scalawags, did their best to create equity-based socioeconomic circumstances for the recently arriving former slaves.

During 1870s and 1880s, as the liberal political power in the state grew stronger, the population of the black neighborhood of Wilmington grew substantially. There were recognizable increases in the number of successful black businesses and the newly established, community financed self-reliance projects particularly in public education and healthcare. However, unfortunately, as the new liberal political reality appeared solidly established in Wilmington, the conservative white supremacist groups remained active behind the scenes at the state level, hoping for a chance to regain political control of North Carolina back into their hands.

One spring day in 1881 Hannah received a letter from Nancy, informing her that George and she finally got married, bought a house and settled near Beale Street. She also wrote that the Greenville plantation no longer existed; it had been taken over by a neighboring plantation.

"*As a result,*" she wrote, "*Mama Rose, the boss of our kitchen in our plantation, moved to Memphis. George and I helped her to start a small barbeque pork eatery business in the black neighborhood. This has turned out to be a very successful partnership. Recently, George left the military and now helps me and Mama Rose run the eatery business.*"

A few years later, Nancy and George visited Hannah and Ned in Wilmington. It was a very special occasion for both couples. Hannah and Ned were very happy to welcome old friends from their plantation days. During a plush dinner party celebrating their reunion, Nancy told her hosts that their life in Memphis was now calm and prosperous.

She added facetiously, "White folks now a days ignore us and we also ignore them right back. So, day by day, life goes on something like that."

"That ain't so!" interjected George. "We colored folks still remain servants of the white folks. Most of them colored folks in our neighborhood work for white folks as cooks, house cleaners, nannies and gardeners. And many of us colored folks work as cheap workers in many white owned factories and businesses. Only a few of us colored folks ain't working for the white folks. That is us, Nancy and me. We're self-employed in Beale Street neighborhood. So, only self-employed negroes like me gonna be ignored by the local white folks."

"It ain't same here, George." Hannah responded. "In Wilmington, there's a calm and respectful attitude toward us colored folks. Even though we ain't living in same neighborhoods, whites and colored folks gonna mingle much more regularly and everybody gonna treat each other with respect and kindness."

"Not only that!" Ned quickly added, "Both communities, colored and white, run the local government of Wilmington in a shared fashion. Even though there's now considerable number of colored folks in Wilmington, many of us unfortunately not allowed to vote yet. Presently there are only a few elected but mostly nominated black members in the Wilmington city council. Similar to the situation in Memphis, in Wilmington most colored folks work in homes and businesses owned by the white community as well. However, one crucial fact remains: as many new businesses in the colored neighborhood develop further, there'll be more jobs for us colored folks to work in our own communities."

George sullenly retorted, "Ain't we colored folks supposed to be free citizens? No, we ain't. In Memphis, like you in Wilmington, we also ain't got the right to vote. But differing from your situation here, we definitely ain't got access to money to borrow for our own needs. The white merchants in Memphis operate with access to borrow money from their white-owned banks. This ain't true for us. We colored folks only gonna use our own hard-earned cash to start new establishments in our colored neighborhoods."

Ned promptly replied, "You're correct, George. We now have a black-owned bank in our colored community, which help newly established colored-owned businesses to borrow money. Furthermore, I hope one day we will have our own newspaper too."

As he laughed, George responded, "Ain't you dreaming Ned? You hope much too much. After establishing a black-owned bank, you gonna now asking for a newspaper owned by colored folks? That'll be the day! I am sure the white folks ain't gonna allow that to happen."

"Why do you say that, George?" asked Ned.

"I just got a gut feeling. We knows Northern liberals won the civil war. But then after killing Lincoln, most of former southern politicians resist local scalawags and the carpetbaggers. Them now gonna gain more and more political control in southern states' legislatures and even at the federal congress. Them political changes ain't gonna bring back slavery but them changes may result in more and more laws and regulations against colored folks to keep us formers slaves not educated and unhealthy so we gonna keep on working as their servants in their homes and as cheap workers in their factories."

"I hope you're wrong George."

"Yeah, I also hope I'm wrong, Ned. But unfortunately, something ain't right about letting us colored slaves be free without giving us right to vote. Also, we former slaves ain't allowed reading and writing. Without access to learning and skills, we ain't got no chance finding work to earn money. How could we colored folks gonna become free citizens while most of us ain't got nothing to eat and ain't got no roof over our head."

This politically sensitive, heated discussion was interrupted when Zahara returned from school.

When Nancy was introduced to Zahara, now called Sarah by her school friends, she was overwhelmed with her natural beauty and the dignified appearance.

As she gave a warm hug to Sarah, Nancy said, "Hannah, your daughter is gonna be a natural beauty and she got a lot of dignity and poise. She gonna be a self-confident and capable young lady. Ain't you teaching her about her African heritage and slave background?"

"Of course, I do! You know, she also got Chickasaw Indian blood. So, I'm telling her about her black African and American Indian background. I also gonna try teaching her about the horrible times of slavery. I always says to her slavery never gonna be repeated and it ain't gonna be forgotten."

A few days after Nancy and George went back to Memphis, Ned grabbed his shotgun out of the bedroom closet. As he was preparing to leave the house, Hannah nervously asked where he was going with a rifle in his hand.

"I forgot to tell you, a few days ago a group of hooded KKK men on horseback attacked a new colored settlement in the northern part of the neighborhood. They burned down a few recently built houses. Yesterday I joined a group of armed colored men to protect our neighborhoods. If the KKK men try to do that again, we'll be there to shoot them down."

"Then what you think gonna happen?" Hannah promptly asked. "If you do that, more of them KKK men come back to punish us. Ain't you forgotten what happened in Memphis?"

With a sullen face, Ned replied, "That was Memphis; this is Wilmington. Many things have changed since then."

"Unfortunately, most of them changes ain't so good for us colored folks. Please, you be very careful."

...

Sarah graduated from High School in 1890. Two years later, she got married to a young, aspiring printing technician named Samuel Brown, who worked at a local newspaper *Wilmington Morning Star*.

Sarah and Sam had a son in 1893; they named him after Ned's father Joseph. Soon after little Joe's birth, with some financial help from Ned and Hannah, they were able to purchase a small house near Hannah's eatery. Before they moved into their house, Ned completely refurbished it.

One early afternoon in the spring of 1894, Sam walked into Hannah's eatery for lunch with a tall, fair-skinned colored man with thick black mustache. He appeared to be in his late twenties. As Hannah welcomed them into the eatery, Sam introduced the man to Hannah as his new boss named Alexander Manly, the owner and head editor of a newly established local newspaper, *The Wilmington Daily*

Record. It would soon to be circulated in Wilmington as the first and only black-owned newspaper in the United States.

Alexander Manly was born in 1866 in Raleigh, North Carolina to a mixed-race family. His grandparents were Charles Manly, the former Governor of North Carolina and Mistress Corinne, a colored slave owned by the governor. After graduating from Hampton University in Virginia with a degree in printing technology, Alex Manley settled in Wilmington in 1894 and established, in partnership with his brother Frank, the town's only black-owned newspaper.

As Hannah placed two full plates of barbequed chicken pieces on the table, she appropriately acknowledged Alexander Manly, who immediately asked Hannah about her husband.

"Sam told me that he is a carpenter. I like to meet him. We need many structural improvements in the building we recently purchased for our newspaper company. Would it be possible for him to visit my office tomorrow morning?"

"Of course, I'm gonna ask him to visit you. Where's your building?"

"Sam knows where it is. He should bring Ned to my office."

"What's my son-in-law gonna do in your office?"

"He'll be responsible for printing and distribution of our daily newspaper."

The next morning, Ned visited Alex Manly in his office. Alex gave him a tour of the building, named *Love and Charity*. Ned noticed that many doors and windows of the old building were in need of repair or replacement. Hearing from Ned that he also owned a furniture store, Alex asked Ned to build a few large tables and chairs for newspaper's meeting rooms. He then asked Ned to join him for a cup coffee in his office.

During their lengthy, friendly discussions, learning that Ned was a blues singer at a local pub, Alex promised him that he would soon come to the pub to listen his blues songs. Afterwards, these two young intellectuals dived heavily into the highly sensitive issues of local politics. Ned stated that Alex's effort to start a black newspaper in Wilmington was an excellent and timely idea.

"Thank you, Ned!" replied Alex. "Wilmington is a fast-developing black community with its own banks, schools, hospitals, and many businesses that are managed by colored middle-class professionals. The two existing local newspapers, *The Wilmington Morning Star* and *The Wilmington Messenger*, are white owned establishments primarily representing the political perspectives of the conservative white community. Unfortunately, most members of this white community have supremacist tendencies. There are clear indications of certain political changes that are about to happen in North Carolina. Since the end of the civil war nearly thirty years ago, the former confederate politicians, who unwillingly accepted the fact that they lost the war but activated political strategies to regain power at the federal, state and municipal legislative levels. In due time, as indicated by the recent election results, the former confederates reached their political aspirations. Local white owned newspapers regularly analyze this ongoing political change process mostly in favor of former confederate's racial mentality that is based on white supremacy. Unfortunately, in the black community of Wilmington, we don't have any press presence representing our perspectives on the ongoing political change and its possible effect on the future of our communities. As the only black newspaper, we will now do our best to reflect on the true nature of our unique African heritage as a countermeasure to many wrong and insulting challenges to our physical as well as cultural existence that were falsely spread by the white racist, segregationist newspapers all over the country. However, as a brand-new publication, we have to rely on the black community's support with their paid subscriptions and advertisements."

Thinking about advertising his own furniture store and Hannah's barbeque chicken eatery, Ned excitedly asked, "When do you plan to start circulation?"

"If all goes well, within a few months' time you will read the first issue."

...

Three months later, *The Wilmington Daily Record*, released its first issue with an introductory editorial comment written by Alexander Manly. In his first editorial piece, he essentially explained the newspaper's primary purpose. He focused on strengthening the voting rights of colored people, provision of better healthcare facilities for the black community and the construction of well-maintained roads in the black neighborhoods.

The first issue of the Wilmington's only colored owned newspaper was full of many local advertisements including Ned's Furniture Store and Hannah's Barbeque Chicken Eatery. Like many of Wilmington's black establishments, the first black owned newspaper also became a sudden success.

During the coming year, Sarah also joined the Wilmington's black newspaper as a typesetter. During her work hours, her four-year-old son Joe was left at home in care of a black nanny. Also during some evenings, when Sam and Sarah went out for entertainment, Ned and Hannah took care of their grandson Joe.

During these prosperous times in Wilmington, Hannah's eatery business did so well that she expanded the capacity of the restaurant from 12 to 24 seats and Ned's furniture store was also expanded due to substantial increases in sales.

...

As years passed, all remained well in the city of Wilmington until the announcement of the results of the municipal elections of November 1898. The announcement created a strong political backlash from the conservative white supremacist sector of the North Carolina's political power base. The conservative, white supremacist Democrat Party had expected to win

OMER ERTUR

elections in all of the municipal jurisdictions in the state including Wilmington. However, as indicated by many statewide elections of the 1890s, primarily due to a statewide economic downturn, many dissatisfied farmers were increasingly voting for the new Populist Party. Eventually, throughout the decade-long elections, the Democrat Party, representing the former confederate politicians, regained control of North Carolina's County and Municipal jurisdictions by fusing with the farmers voting for the Populist Party. The only exception to this situation happened in Wilmington, the most populated municipality. There, the municipal election of November of 1898 resulted in a victory for the liberal Republican candidates, who successfully joined hands with the local component of the Populist Party, therefore capturing the mayoral post and a clear majority of the city council positions.

The liberal electoral victory in Wilmington created an unstable political stage that became ripe for a forced political takeover of Wilmington's elected municipal government by a violent uprising that would be conducted by red-shirt wearing, armed members of the white supremacist Democrat Party. Now, due to their statewide victories, the Democrat Party members became overly confident and considered venturing into

116

such a risky political activity as forced takeover. Furthermore, because feeling assured of Federal Government's non-interference due to high number of elected segregationist Southern politicians in the United States Congress, the members of the white supremacist Democrat Party searched for an excuse that would create a white supremacist public reaction through which they could successfully accomplish a coup d'état to overtake the newly elected municipal government of Wilmington.

In the summer of 1898, Rebecca Ann Felton, a well-known Georgian writer and political activist supporting women's suffrage, made a racially charged comment in a public speech. She stated that public lynching of a black men who sexually assaulted a white woman was the correct and most appropriate punishment.

The Chief Editor of Wilmington's only black-owned newspaper, *The Daily Record*, responded to Mrs. Felton's white supremacist speech by publishing a well-written editorial that heavily ridiculed Felton's speech by exposing its imbalanced racist rationale. In his editorial, Alex Manly emphasized that it was a natural sexual response for both black and white men to be attracted to females of other races. Furthermore, he wrote that it was appropriate for a white woman to be attracted to a black man and possibly fall in love. Finally, Alex Manly stated that public lynching of a black man, who only revealed his carnal interest in a white woman, was illegal and should never be allowed to happen.

Being born to mixed-race parents, Alex Manly was speaking from his heart. His grandfather, Charles Manly, a former Governor of North Carolina in late 1840s had a carnal relationship with his young slave servant Corinne. Upon her becoming pregnant, he had taken proper legal action to have his last name given to his mixed-race child. Fully aware of the details of his own family background, Alex Manly wrote his editorial piece with a proper understanding and well-supported logic pertaining to the sensitive issue at hand. Unfortunately, Manly, without realizing it, had provided the excuse the white supremacist politicians were searching for. They could now carry out their plans to forcibly takeover the municipality and depose the duly elected multi-racial government of Wilmington.

In the coming days, there were many politically charged, heated reactions to the editorial article written by Alex Manly that appeared in several white supremacist newspapers asking for his lynching. Delighted with what was happening, Democrat Party leaders decided to wait for the results of the November 8, 1898 municipal elections before supporting any mob violence or public lynchings to take place.

Before the election, a Democrat Party rally in Wilmington was sponsored by the white supremacist campaign organized by Alfred M. Waddell, a former congressman and a confederate general. As the keynote speaker Waddell provided the marching orders to a large crowd with the support of Furnifold Simmons, a United States Congressman representing North Carolina.

At that meeting, Waddell loudly claimed, "You are the sons of noble ancestry. You are Anglo-Saxons. You are now well-armed to do your duty in the coming election. Tomorrow, go to the polls and if you see a negro out voting, ask him to leave. If he refuses, kill him; shoot him down on his tracks."

Disregarding these serious threats, many colored folks and a considerable number of whites in Wilmington voted in favor of Republican candidates. When the results of the November 8 election in Wilmington were not in their favor, the Democrat Party leadership decided to proceed with the planned white supremacist riot against the Wilmington's black-owned newspaper. They further planned that the street riots would be followed by a coup d'état against the duly elected multiracial municipal government of Wilmington.

On 9th of November, the day after the election, the white-owned newspaper, *The Wilmington Messenger*, published the '*White Declaration of Independence*': a list of resolutions including that white men would never be ruled by men of African origin. This declaration also demanded that Alexander Manly must leave the city within 24 hours or he will be lynched.

Learning that his life was under threat and he might be lynched, on the evening of November 9, Alexander Manly together with his family secretly left Wilmington for an unknown location.

Unfortunately, most employees of the newspaper, not yet aware of their boss' departure, came to work during the morning of the bloody racist riot that destroyed the entire newspaper building and killed many of the workers inside.

On November 10, 1898, thousands of white supremacist rioters led by armed party members in red shirts were congregated in the streets of Wilmington, most of them in front of the black-owned newspaper *The Daily Record*. As these street demonstrations against the black-owned newspaper of Wilmington continued, racist politicians who had lost the recent election in Wilmington decided to take over the municipal government. At the same time, they took a decision to allow the rioters to destroy the black-owned newspaper building and all other prominent black businesses of Wilmington.

Early morning of that ominous day, Joe's nanny did not show up to take care of him. Sarah decided to drop his son at his parents' house on her way to work. Reaching the house, she told her mother Joe's nanny did not show up.

"Mom, streets in downtown aren't safe. There were many red-shirts with guns in front of our building last night. I hope all this nonsense will soon go away. But I think you should keep your eatery closed today. Stay home or go to father's shop for the rest of the day. I will pick Joe up after work. If you aren't here, I'll come to dad's workshop."

After Sarah's departure, Ned came to the kitchen to have his breakfast. Noticing his grandson Joe in the kitchen eating a bowl of cereal, he asked Hannah what was going on. Hannah told him about the riots in the city. Ned then suggested the same thing Sarah had told her mother, that they should come to his workshop.

"Our home and your eatery are very close to the newspaper building where most of the white supremacist rioters would gather. I think it's safer for us if we stay in my workshop until the police put down the rioting."

With a disturbed look on her face, Hannah replied, "Ned, I got a really bad feeling. This rioting ain't gonna end well for us colored folks. Like we did thirty-two years ago in Memphis, I hope we ain't gonna hide again."

Before noon, they left the house for Ned's workshop several blocks away from the downtown. As they were walking, they could hear gunshots a few blocks away. Holding little Joe's hand tightly, Hannah loudly asked Ned, "Do you think Sarah and Sam gonna be safe at the newspaper?"

"I'm sure the police presence would prevent the rioters attacking the newspaper. I also hope a few state troopers will soon come to Wilmington to stop the ongoing rioting."

They safely reached to Ned's workshop but they were not aware of what had happened a short while earlier in the municipal government building. Because of a successful coup d'état, the duly-elected mayor, Silas Wright, had been deposed and the police chief, George French, had been replaced. The new white supremacist mayor Alfred M. Waddell and his self-appointed police chief did not order the police to protect the black-owned newspaper building and the personnel inside. Contrarily, they ordered the police force to support the red-shirted Democrat Party members leading the racist crowd.

Soon after that order issued by the new police chief, the red-shirted party members and the white supremacist mob entered the newspaper building and attacked the personnel inside. After burning the newspaper building down and killing most of the workers, the hundreds of white rioters attacked and burned down many black-owned businesses and homes in Wilmington's black neighborhood, including Hannah's eatery, and the houses Ned built for his family and his daughter Sarah's family.

During the rest of the morning, over three hundred black residents of Wilmington were killed by the rioters. Many blacks, who were descendants of former slaves, trusted the government and worked hard to reach to a socio-economic level in par with their former slave owning white masters. They were killed in cold blood by fully armed white supremacists representing the mindset of the former confederates.

By early afternoon, the bloodthirsty mob was getting close to Ned's workshop. Hearing gunshots and smelling the smoke from burning houses a block away, Ned quickly packed a few blankets he had in the shop and grabbed a jug of water to leave before the rioters got any closer.

"Where we gonna go?" asked Hannah nervously.

"Do you remember the large colored folks' cemetery two blocks north of our house? We were there a few months ago for a burial service. We should hide there until the violence ends."

That is exactly what they did. Like hundreds of colored folks who escaped from their homes and businesses, Ned, Hannah and their grandson little Joe Brown, took refuge in the vast black cemetery of Wilmington.

The next morning, thousands of colored folks including the ones hiding in the cemetery were taken to the train station by the police and forced into empty train wagons to leave the state of North Carolina for good. These colored folks' final destinations would be determined by the amount of cash they had in their pockets, that is if they had any inkling about where they could go. Many of those who could not pay for the train ride were thrown off the trains outside the North Carolina state border. Many of those colored folks suffered tremendously and most of them possibly perished after they were taken off the wagons as they tried walking to unknown distant destinations in the middle of the winter.

As the bloodthirsty coup d'état in Wilmington, supported by the North Carolina State political apparatus, had been successfully completed, the United States Federal Government had chosen to completely disregard this tragic political affair as if it never had happened. The clear losers of this bloody race riot were the colored folks of Wilmington, who in cooperation with their liberal white neighbors, was able to established a thriving, self-sufficient multi-racial community. As a consequence of this racist, supremacist uprising, the colored folks of Wilmington lost all what they owned, many of them were killed, their houses and businesses were destroyed and many survivors were forced out of the State of North Carolina and their losses were never acknowledged or compensated.

The bloody political overthrow of the duly elected bi-racial local government of Wilmington in North Carolina was the beginning of Jim Crow laws that were introduced in many of the states that established the legal concept of separation of black and white communities in all aspects of public life under the 1896 United States Supreme Court decision titled "*Separate but Equal*".

As a result of that Supreme Court ruling, all of the segregated black communities became definitely separate; but in terms of quality of life, they were never given any chance to become equal to the white communities' standards of living. In comparison to the neighboring white communities, a black community was never able to improve its living standards enough to establish a thriving middle class. However, if and when a black community became wealthy and self-sufficient, the white supremacist mobs destroyed it without any mercy, as it happened in Memphis, Tennessee in 1866 and in Wilmington, North Carolina in 1898.

Since there were no official investigation of the white supremacist uprising in Wilmington, no one was able to identify anyone of the unfortunate newspaper workers who were killed that day. Resultantly, Ned and Hannah never learned about what had happened to Sarah and Sam. Their names, like the names of the colored folks murdered during that ominous day, completely disappeared into the governmental void created by the white supremacist politicians representing the dark mindset of racist former confederate states. Though they definitely lost the civil war but in time, the former confederate states gained immense political power in many southern states' legislatures and in the United States Federal Congress.

After crying silently for many hours in the crowded compartment of the slow-moving train, Hannah turned to Ned.

"Where're we gonna go now?"

Ned, with a forced smile on his tired face, held her hand tightly.

"One of the guitar players in my blues band was from Springfield, Illinois. He told me that there was a great number of pubs with live music in the town's black neighborhood just like Beale Street in Memphis.

I might get a job in one of those pubs for us to have a fresh start."

"Why ain't you gonna do carpentry work?" asked Hannah hastily.

"All my tools are destroyed. It'll be very expensive for me to get a new set of tools. But I think I can buy a cheap used guitar to start performing at a local pub immediately."

"I'm so sorry, Ned! You ain't got the guitar your father made for you."

After remaining silent a short while, she suddenly remarked, "I ain't gonna stop worrying about Sarah and Sam. You think they're all right?"

Looking at his grandson lovingly, Ned replied, "I pray the Lord they survived the upheavals of that horrible day and by now, they are safe in their home."

It took many days for Hannah and Ned to reach the state of Illinois because in many train stations they had to wait to change into trains with proper track gauge. Finally, they arrived at their destination of Springfield, Illinois. As they got off the train, Ned told Hannah that Illinois was the birth state of Lincoln.

Hannah responded with facetious comment, "So what?"

Ned quickly replied, "I think this small town might be the appropriate place for us to raise our grandson."

Ned was not yet aware of how wrong he was about Springfield. With the arrival of many new immigrants from Europe, mostly the Irish and Italians who were aggressively competing for scarce local jobs also available for the colored workers, strong racist sentiments were brewing in the white communities of Springfield. Most of the newly arrived white immigrants to the city became, in time, intolerant racists. Due to immigration of many Europeans, by late 1898 the black component of Springfield's population had been reduced to less than three percent.

Springfield, Illinois

Soon after getting a room in a small hotel in the black neighborhood of Springfield, Ned went out to shop for a used guitar. Soon he found a used guitar in good shape. He immediately started searching for a singing job in local pubs. A few days later, he joined a blues band playing in a busy pub and started performing during the weekend evenings. After his first night's earnings, he rented an apartment near the pub.

Looking after her grandson Joe, Hannah was not able to seek employment nearly for a year until little Joe would start attending elementary school. Settling into her tiny apartment, Hannah wrote letters to friends in Wilmington seeking information about Sarah and Sam. A few weeks later, she only received a reply from Dollie, the wife of the lumberyard owner Philip. Dollie wrote that no one in the police department was willing to release information about what happened to the Newspaper workers during the racist uprising. Dollie added that no one had seen Sarah or Sam since the uprising. Therefore, she concluded, it could be assumed that they did not survive the bloody attacks. She ended her letter with a declaration that two businesses Ned and Hannah owned and the houses that belonged to them and their daughter Sarah were completely destroyed by the racist crowd.

...

Little Joe Brown started attending elementary school in early September of 1899. By late January 1900, Ned was able purchase a few essential tools and found a part-time job in a carpentry workshop. Hannah was also now fully employed at a local barbeque ribs eatery as a cook's assistant. They now earned enough income to live comfortably and provide a secure home and good education for their grandson Joe. Unfortunately, they were not able to forget their wealthy and comfortable lifestyle in Wilmington that had been suddenly and tragically terminated. But, worst of it all, they lost their much-loved daughter Sarah and her beloved husband Sam.

In many occasions, remembering their journeys from Greenville to Memphis and from Memphis to Wilmington, Ned and Hannah reminisced about all the good things that had happened to them in their lifelong struggle to survive the injustices of a racist social reality they were forced to accept since the end of the civil war. But what had happened in Wilmington was not something that could easily be rationalized and accepted. They tried to put out of their minds but it was not possible because they lost their much-loved daughter. Now, surviving in this little industrial town's small black neighborhood surrounded by not so friendly racist white folks, their most basic purpose in life was to simply raise their grandson Joe in a proper way. They were able to place their grandson in the only private school that allowed black children to attend for a considerably high tuition.

It took Hannah almost two years to finally accept the tragedy that resulted in demise of her daughter and son-in-law. She finally wrote a long letter to Nancy informing her that they were now in Springfield, Illinois. It was excruciatingly painful for Hannah to write a few lines about Sarah and Sam's deaths.

A month later, she received Nancy's reply. In her letter Nancy expressed the sorrow she felt about the tragic news. She wrote that what happened in Wilmington did not appear in any of the local newspapers in Memphis. She then added that George had been in prison during the past several months for punching a white policeman and that he might be released from prison in two years' time.

Nearly two years later, Nancy wrote Hannah that George was now out of prison. In that letter Nancy also wrote about the death of Mama Rose.

"Because of her death," she wrote, *"I am now fully in charge of the kitchen in our eatery."*

She ended her letter by complaining about the establishment of separate toilets and drinking fountains for colored folks in Memphis' public areas commonly frequented by both races.

Later part of that year, Hannah was not surprised when the Springfield municipality also activated similar Jim Crow laws requiring the establishment of separate toilets and drinking water fountains only for the colored folks in designated public areas.

•••

After many uneventful years, at the beginning of the summer of the year 1908, Joe Brown, now 14 years old young adult, graduated from the private junior high school. Attending the graduation ceremony of their grandson was a joyful occasion for Hannah and Ned; they were proud of little Joe.

Ned and Hannah were now at a crossroad about Joe's further education. They constantly searched for a high school with good reputation for Joe to attend. Not finding a nearby private high school that accepted a black student, Ned started asking around. From a customer in the pub, he learned about the existence of a prominent black neighborhood with a reputable public high school in Tulsa, Oklahoma. He discussed it with Hannah and they decided to move to Tulsa before the end of summer.

On 13 August 1908, in the late hours of the evening, a drunk black man entered a bedroom of a white-owned house where two young girls were asleep in their beds. Waking up to his children's screams, their father chased the intruder out of his house. Outside the house he was able to catch the intoxicated man. They started to fight. The colored man stabbed the white man and ran away but was soon caught by police officers. He was immediately arrested and placed in jail. The wounded white man unfortunately died the following morning. The colored man in jail was charged with murder.

The news of this violent affair quickly spread all over Springfield's white neighborhoods. In the morning of August 14, hearing about a white man was killed by a colored man as he defended his young, virgin daughters, a large number of white rioters took to the streets. With the intention to lynch the rapist murderer, the angry mob went straight to the jail where the colored man was being held. Fortunately, expecting the rioter's arrival at the jail, the police smuggled the suspect to another jail.

Reaching the jail and not finding the colored man to lynch, the mob decided to attack the colored folks living in the nearby black neighborhood. That afternoon, armed white rioters viciously attacked and killed many colored folks on the streets and destroyed many black-owned businesses and houses.

This violent, bloody racist uprising in Springfield, Illinois lasted for three days during which several blacks were killed and many black establishments, including the pub Ned had performed, were completely destroyed.

On August 15, without any hesitation, Ned, Hannah and Joe packed a few of their essential personal items, walked to the station and took the first available train out of Springfield.

On the train Hannah asked Ned, "Ain't we full citizens of this country? If so, why such hatred and violence allowed against us colored folks? Why white folks who fought to free us now allowing such terrible violence against us colored folks to take place?"

"After the civil war," Ned replied, "we were emancipated immediately. For that reason, we are no longer slaves but free people. Unfortunately, such a forced emancipation was not accepted by many white folks living in the southern states. They just did not want to share their living space with us colored folks as free people. So, they were only willing to allow us to exist in our miserable neighborhoods as long as we provided cheap labor for maintaining their homes and gardens and working in their businesses and factories as underpaid laborers. But, when we were able to establish self-sufficient black-run communities, they did not like it and they did their best to destroy our homes and businesses as they did in Memphis in 1866, in Wilmington ten years ago and now in Springfield."

"Ain't there a legal way to prevent racist violence against us colored folks?"

"Yes, there would have been a judicial possibility to curtail white racist attacks against the black people if the United States Congress and the Supreme Court, using its inherent constitutional powers, enacted legal procedures to prevent such violent actions against black communities from occurring and reoccurring. Quite the opposite, during the past decade many Jim Crow segregationist laws were enacted in many southern states to further segregate colored communities and prevent colored people from equal access to certain public facilities such as toilets, restaurants and forcing the colored folks to sit separately in rear sections of the public transport facilities such as busses and trams. By the way, such segregationist regulations were never considered by the bi-racially managed Wilmington City Council. But in time, many states including a few of the northern states, blacks were discriminated against in using many public facilities. In 1896, all these segregation-based discriminations against colored people were taken to the Supreme Court. Unfortunately, the Supreme Court decided that such actions to segregate whites and blacks were based on *'separate but equal'* principle, therefore they were constitutionally acceptable measures."

"I don't understand the reasons behind such racist decisions forcing us to use separate toilets. We are all human beings, ain't we. However, I get the reason why they wanna legalize segregation of coloreds and whites. They wanna allow us to have our own neighborhoods. But when we work hard and establish separate and independent communities with its our own schools, health services and banks, the white folks viciously attack and destroy our communities. That ain't make any sense to me! So, now tell me why you think our life's gonna be any better in this new town we gonna move?"

"I am not sure that it would be any better but I am sure that it won't be any worse! We just have to hope for the best and move on with our lives."

"To what end we gonna do that?"

Looking affectionately at his grandson Joe, Ned calmly replied, "We have to raise our grandchild in a safe town with a good school."

The train ride to Tulsa took many days because they frequently had to change trains due to track size differences at several train stations. As they got closer to Oklahoma, Hannah noticed that the train was passing through endlessly dry flatlands in the mid-western part of the United States.

Pointing at the horizon, Hannah commented, "Ned, you think Oklahoma flat and dry like this?"

Glancing out of the window, Ned replied, "I presume it would be quite similar. We'll see how flat it is when we get there. Just to let you know that Oklahoma became a state hardly a year ago. The discovery of petroleum in 1897 on Oklahoma's Indian territories apparently stimulated the establishment and growth of Tulsa. I also heard that Tulsa originally started as an outpost of Creek Indians."

"You think your mother's Chickasaw tribe also forced to move to Oklahoma?"

"It is highly probable that the whole tribe settled somewhere in Oklahoma. We'll find out when we get there."

Noticing a weird looking, tall iron structure that appeared over the horizon, Hannah asked, "What is that?"

"I think that is an oil-well."

"What an oil-well do?"

"It just sucks petroleum out of the ground. Before you ask, I'll tell you what it's good for. Petroleum is a liquid that burns quickly and it may be used in heating homes and running some industrial machinery."

Ned's comments about petroleum were to the point. Since Oklahoma had become the 46th state in 1907, Tulsa had grown exponentially due to the arrivals of railroads and the financiers who were chasing after the immense wealth created by the oil industry. During the early part of the 20th century, Tulsa became one of the oil capitals of the world. The city's growth was clearly visible as the urban skyline had blossomed with many buildings and, at the same time, its population doubled in size.

Tulsa, Oklahoma

A few days later, they arrived at Tulsa early in the morning. Hannah was the first to get off the train. As she waited on the platform for Ned and Joe, she intensely looked around. Immediately she became disappointed with Tulsa's dusty and flat urban scenery. As they walked toward the black neighborhood across the railroad, she asked Ned, "I ain't so sure this is the town we gonna live and raise our grandson?"

"Don't you worry Hannah. In time, its appearance will improve. I believe, since this is a fast-growing town, we'll have plenty of opportunities to establish your eatery business and my carpentry shop."

"You ain't gonna sing your songs no more? I ain't sure there's a drinking pub in this dusty small town for you to sing your blue songs?"

"I'm sure there are many drinking places in this town because our folk music will always be heard in places where negroes gather to drink and have a good time. Let's quickly find a place to settle for the evening. Afterwards, we should find a place to eat. I'm starving!"

They soon noticed a large street sign announcing rooms for rent on the front yard of a big wooden house at the main street of the black neighborhood named Greenwood. They quickly rented a room at Damie Rowland's Boarding House. After placing their luggage in the room, they went out to find a place to eat. Finding a small eatery specializing in barbequed ribs, they quickly ate their early supper and went back to their room to sleep until next morning to recover from the weeklong train voyage.

The next morning, they talked to the landlady named Miss Damie about the location of a school for Joe. She told them where the school was. They immediately went to the Booker T. Washington High School and a short while later they happily walked their grandson into a classroom full of black 9th graders.

Ned and Hannah spent the rest of the day walking around the town. They were pleased to discover many different shops that sold many essential items they would need to start their new life in Tulsa. Noticing a hardware store, Ned went in to see their stock of carpentry tools. Discovering the store had most of the quality *Stanley* carpentry tools, he excitedly looked at Hannah.

"As soon as I find a large house to rent, I'll buy a new set of carpentry tools to establish my workshop."

As they continued walking around the main street, Hannah noticed that there were greater number of automobiles in the black neighborhood of Tulsa than she had seen in the Springfield's black neighborhood. When she mentioned that fact to Ned, he replied, "Because Springfield's black neighborhood is a very poor place. Unemployed or underemployed poor black folks in Springfield can't purchase these expensive automobiles. That is the reason we did not see any cars around our neighborhood in Springfield. But here Tulsa, it seems black folks are a bid wealthier. Because of that reason, some of them are able to afford these very expensive automobiles."

"Do you think we gonna purchase an automobile one day?"

"We could do that if we have enough money. But for now, I think we should find a horse buggy for us to travel around the town."

"Like we did in Memphis and Wilmington."

"Exactly, but first we have to find a house for us to move into as soon as possible."

Soon after he completed his sentence, he noticed an animal feed shop. In front of the shop, a large, heavyset brown skinned man with pony-tailed long hair stood still as he smoked a cigarette and watched the horse carriages and a few noisy automobiles pass him by. Ned approached him and introduced himself. He told him he was interested in buying a used horse buggy.

The large man promptly introduced himself, "My name is Big John. I am the owner of this store. I have a few customers who might consider selling one of their old carriages."

Big John asked Ned to come back in a few days so he could provide the name of the person who might consider selling his old carriage. Ned agreed to come back but then quickly asked, "Are you a Chickasaw?"

"Yes, I am. Why do you ask?"

"I am half Chickasaw and half Negro. My grandfather was the Great Chief Tishomingo."

Looking at both Ned and Hannah with a wide grin on his brown face, Big John, softly remarked, "I occasionally visit my tribal relatives in Chickasaw reservation. Next week I am planning to go there. Would you and your lady like to join me? We can also visit the sacred ground where your grandfather Tishomingo is buried."

That was the beginning of a long-lasting friendship between Ned Blum and Big John, who promised that he would soon introduce Ned to an owner of a horse barn to buy a horse for his future carriage.

The next morning Big John took Ned and Hannah to the horse barn owned by a Cherokee named Slim Jim, a tall, skinny, brown skinned man with straggly long white hair. As Ned was carefully inspecting the horses in the barn, the Cherokee man, learning about Ned's Chickasaw and Negro background, told him that if he wanted to buy a house, he should meet the half Indian half negro man named Hezekiah White, who owned large tracts of land and many properties near Greenwood Avenue. Ned thanked him for the information and told Slim Jim he would buy one of his horses soon after he finds himself a used carriage.

After a nearly a week-long search, with the help of Hezekiah White, who appeared to know everyone in Greenwood, Ned and Hannah located an old two-floor wooden house on one of the back streets of the main avenue. The house was large enough for Ned to build a carpentry workshop in the first floor of the house. They bought the house and immediately moved into the second floor. Ned quickly built a separate bedroom for Joe on the second floor.

Unfortunately, there were two specific problems about the house immensely bothered Hannah: the kitchen was too small and the outhouse in the backyard was too far away. Ned promised Hannah that he would soon fix these two problems that made her unhappy about the house.

A day later, Ned, Hannah and Joe joined Big John for a day long horse-carriage ride to the Chickasaw Reservation. They were welcomed by Chickasaw tribal members as if they were royalty. After spending the night in a teepee for the first time in their lives, next morning they were taken to the sacred burial ground.

On the way, the Chickasaw Chief asked Ned if he could speak any Chikashshanompa, the language of the Chickasaw. After uttering a few words that he could remember from his mother, Ned apologized for not speaking it well. Switching back to English, the Chief asked Big John to translate the prayers that he soon would utter for the soul of Great Chief Tishomingo, Ned's maternal grandfather.

After the special prayer conducted by the tribal leader, they spent the afternoon sitting around a bonfire and smoking tobacco with wooden pipes. At that meeting Ned and Hannah learned about how hospitable and helpful the Chickasaw tribesmen were toward the escaped slaves before and during the civil war.

"Also, after the civil war," the tribal chief commented, "we helped many freed former slaves to settle on our tribal lands to become farmers."

On the way back to Tulsa, Ned told Joe that he should be proud of his Chickasaw heritage. Hannah, quickly added that Joe should also be proud of his African heritage.

After he brought all the necessary carpentry tools, Ned started to build many types of household furniture to sell. In the meantime, he decided to teach woodwork to his grandson Joe. After school hours, Joe joined his grandfather in the workshop and learned how to handle various tools to repair damaged furniture and how to make brand new furniture pieces. Joe, as he learned carpentry from his grandfather, was very happy indeed with his new high school and the grades he received clearly indicated that fact.

They now had a house to live in and a carpentry workshop for Ned to earn income. With the assistance of Big John, Ned bought an old horse buggy and soon after that Ned purchased a horse from Slim Jim. Now, with a new horse-buggy to go around the town, they were about to reach their former comfortable lifestyle they had in Wilmington. The only thing that remained missing was a place for Hannah to start her eatery business on Greenwood Avenue. It took Ned a while to find a property at a proper location for an eatery that would generate profit. When a small old house became available in the center of the Greenwood Avenue near recently opened Stratford Hotel and the large grocery store, Ned took Hannah to the house for her approval. Upon her agreement, they purchased the house. A month later, after Ned completely refurbished the old house and converted it to an eatery, Hannah's barbeque chicken restaurant with six tables serving only lunch had opened for business in early 1910. It became an immediate business success.

Soon after opening the Hannah's eatery, Ned joined a group of musicians performing blues songs at the famous Little Bell Café. It was situated in the entertainment section of the Greenwood neighborhood called *Little Africa that was* frequently visited by many white Tulsans. Apparently, ongoing segregation policies did not prohibit whites from patronizing black establishments in Greenwood.

Nearly a year later, after being involved into many ongoing building construction activities, Ned opened his own construction firm office near the busy part of Greenwood Avenue. He moved the carpentry workshop and all of his tools to his new office. After moving the workshop away from the house, Ned reconstructed the first floor of the house to meet Hannah's expectations. Hannah was very happy indeed with the new living room, enlarged kitchen, and indoor water-closet with running water.

A day after receiving the furniture for the new living room, Hannah prepared a special dinner for Ned to celebrate the occasion. That afternoon, after closing the eatery, she stopped by nearby grocery store and purchased a bottle of imported red French wine and two elegant wine glasses. That evening after eating the sumptuous dinner and drinking the whole bottle of wine, they walked out hand-in-hand to the front porch. Sitting side by side on the large swinging chair, they reminisced.

Glancing lovingly at Ned, her partner for life, Hannah murmured, "You know sweetheart, after three

OMER ERTUR

failed attempts to find a safe and secure town to live, we finally got a place that's gonna be fine for the time being. You know, if ever our living here in Greenwood disrupted by violence, we both ain't young enough to search for a new place to settle."

Staring at her worriedly, Ned replied, "I don't understand why you suddenly feel so insecure? I believe all is well here in Tulsa."

"To you, it's gonna sound a bit strange but in my mind, I always compare Tulsa's Greenwood black community to Wilmington's bi-racial community where we colored folks co-existed peacefully with the white folks. Unfortunately, I ain't got no feeling that kind of respectful living gonna be realized here in Tulsa."

"What makes you to say these words, Hannah?"

"In Wilmington's public areas, there ain't any separate toilets and water fountains for only colored people to use. But here in Tulsa's white neighborhoods, there're toilets and drinking water fountains only for us colored folks. I also remember, in Wilmington we got black-owned banks. Here in Greenwood, we ain't got any black-owned bank. I have to go to the white-owned *Exchange National Bank* to deposit my eatery's earnings. Many colored folks work for white folks as house servants, gardeners and many work in white-

152

owned businesses or factories. But I ain't allowed to hire a white girl to work in my eatery and you ain't also allowed to hire a white worker for your construction. I don't understand, if many things ain't possible for neither of us to do, how this gonna be interpreted as *'separate but equal'*?"

"I fully understand your concerns. I think, in time many of these things may be corrected and both communities may finally accept each other. I heard a rumor that soon we'll have our own newspaper like we had in Wilmington."

Suddenly looking extremely solemn and concerned, Hannah replied, "It ain't possible that you forgot what happened to that newspaper in Wilmington. We lost our daughter and son-in-law in that damn newspaper. I simply ain't gonna agree with your hopeful outlook. I ain't seeing such capacity for goodness in most white people. They ain't gonna clear their minds of racism and accept us colored folks as human beings. I ain't believing no longer we colored folks gonna be living in peace with white folks. I believes such wishful thinking's just an empty dream that's gonna turn into a horrible nightmare here in Tulsa like it was in Wilmington."

153

Ned could not find words to respond to Hannah's highly critical comments about Tulsa; so, he kept silent. That night, as he kept on thinking about Hannah's strong words, he remained awake most of the night.

A few weeks later, Hannah received a letter from Nancy about George's death from a sudden heart attack. *"Without George,"* she wrote, *"I'm no longer gonna manage the eatery."* Nancy ended the letter saying that she would soon sell the business.

Hannah immediately wrote back and asked her to consider moving to Tulsa.

"If you like it here, you're gonna stay with us. Life here in Tulsa is calm and enjoyable."

A few weeks later, she received her reply. In the letter Nancy wrote that after selling the eatery, she'll take the train to Tulsa. Hardly a week later, she also received a telegram from Nancy that she was on her way to Tulsa. Hannah immediately prepared a room for her dear friend.

Nancy, carrying one small luggage, showed up in Hannah's eatery during a warm April day in 1915. Soon after her arrival in Tulsa, she became an invaluable member of Hannah's family. Hardly a month later, Nancy joined Hannah in the eatery and her specially baked Mississippi mudpies became a favorite of the customers.

One late Saturday evening Hannah and Nancy went to the Little Bell Café to listen to Ned perform with a blues group. Ned, noticing Hannah and Nancy among the audience sitting at the bar, announced that he would sing one of his blues compositions titled *The Wings of Freedom,* named by his wife Hannah presently in the audience.

This very melodic but sad song about slavery brought Nancy and Hannah to tears.

Holding Hannah's hand, Nancy murmured, "As slaves we got a lot of suffering; ain't we?"

"Yes, indeed we did but I ain't sure that our sufferings ended with emancipation."

"Why you say such a thing, Hannah? All seems fine here in Tulsa."

"It ain't a true appearance; it's false. We colored folks gonna be allowed to remain in this separate neighborhood as long as we do what we're told. Did you notice tonight there're few white folks in the café? Rarely, white folks come to our eatery to taste our barbeque chicken. But that ain't true for us

Negroes. We ain't allowed to go to a white neighborhood in Tulsa to listen white-folks' music or taste their food at their restaurants? No, we definitely ain't allowed! To white folks, we ain't matter; we gonna remain their slaves. We ain't got no chance to change white folks' racist feelings because we got no say so, as Ned says we aint got political power to change this horrible situation. To protect ourself and our families we got to remain silent and remain as them whites' servants."

Nancy, appearing solemn, replied, "You got it right, Hannah; I feel exactly the same."

...

During the summer of 1915, Joe graduated from high school and in 1916, he decided to join the military. Since United States was not expected to get involved militarily into the ongoing war in Europe, Ned and Hannah did not object to their grandson joining the army.

After receiving a long and intense training in a boot camp in Charlotte, N.C., Joe's colored division was shipped to France immediately after the United States declared war against Germany in 1917.

During his training in Charlotte, Joe had regularly written many detailed letters to his grandparents. However, while in France nearly for a six-months he did not communicate with his grandparents. Finally, he wrote them a very long letter. In the letter, he informed Ned and Hannah that he was near the front lines but he was not allowed to fight in the trench warfare. Apparently, most of the colored troops were not permitted to involve into the actual fighting. Colored soldiers were mostly used in providing assistance in delivering essential military supplies to fighting men in the trenches. In many occasions, colored soldiers were also used to dig new trenches, clean latrines and bury dead soldiers.

A few months later, Joe wrote another long letter letting his grandparents know that he had been transferred to a colored detachment based near Paris. He was very happy with the warm welcome he had received from the French people.

He wrote: *"The French people's attitude toward us colored folks is very different from how badly we're treated by the white folks in the United States. Somehow, the French people don't seem to notice our dark skin color."*

After the American involvement into the European war effort has ended, most of the white doughboys were immediately released and sent home. However, most of the colored soldiers, including Joe, were transferred to a colored detachment at Camp McClellan in Anniston, Alabama. It took many more months of waiting for the colored soldiers to receive their honorable discharges. As they conducted many hours of guard duty, they patiently waited to be released from the military and worked hard in many daily maintenance and cleaning toils.

One day, after completing his guard duty at the camp's main entry post, Joe wrote another long letter to his grandparents, telling them about a disturbing incident that had occurred at the military base:

"I was on guard duty when my sergeant Edgar Caldwell, in full army uniform, left the base before noon for a furlough at the nearby town called Hobson City. Hardly three hours later, he came rushing back into the guard post. Trying to catch his breath, the sergeant ordered me to remain silent when police officers arrive at the guard post. I asked him what happened. He told me that he killed two white men in Hobson City. When I asked why, he hurriedly told me that when he got into a tram, the driver called him a nigger boy and ordered him to move to the back of the vehicle. He responded to

the driver by stating that he was a returning war veteran and warned him that he should be respectful toward a man in army uniform. Against all of his appeals, the driver still cussed at him and told him to shut up and move to tram's rear section. Sergeant Caldwell lost his temper and punched the driver. Noticing the ongoing violent conflict in front section of the tram, the driver's assistant rushed toward them. Two white men fought the Sergeant and pushed him off the tram. Outside the tram, Sergeant tried walking away from them. But the driver and his assistant chased after him and kept on punching him viciously. So, the sergeant took out his gun and shot them both dead. he then ran away back to the army base. I reminded him that he should immediately report this incident to the officer-in-charge. Sergeant Caldwell did exactly that. Together with the officer-in-charge they reported what happened in Dobson City to the commander of the colored troops at the army base. Hardly an hour later, the Sheriff of Hobson City followed by two state trooper vehicles arrived at the base and asked me to inform the commanding officer that they were there to arrest the Sergeant. Soon after I informed the commander, he came to the guard post and flatly refused to turn the Sergeant over to the law *enforcement officers. He told them that in regards to Sergeant Caldwell's presumed crime, the military authorities were responsible to investigate the situation and according to the rules of military justice, they would take necessary legal action against the Sergeant. As this was going on, I heard from the police officers waiting in front of the guard post that there was a large crowd of people in Hobson city waiting on the streets to lynch the Sergeant."*

Three months later, Joe Brown was honorably discharged from the US Army and came home to Tulsa. Joe's safe return from his military duties resulted in an exciting homecoming family celebration that included Nancy.

The next morning during breakfast, Ned asked Joe about the fate of his sergeant. Joe replied, "I heard some rumors before I left Camp McClellan. Because of the mitigating circumstances, the Sergeant may not be charged with murder of the tram driver. The driver's deputy was wounded but survived. It seems the Sergeant might soon be released back into civilian life."

Hearing that, Ned turned to Hannah.

"Isn't that nice that the military justice protected the Sergeant?"

Looking calm and unimpressed, Hannah commented, "Where was the military justice when hundreds of colored folks gotten killed in Memphis, Wilmington and Springfield? Me thinks the colored Sergeant gonna be thankful to his commanding officer. He saved sergeant from a lynching white crowd."

A few days later, Ned informed Hannah about his decision to buy a new car directly from Detroit, Michigan. When Hannah threw a questioning look at Ned, he simply told her that they could now afford to buy a car because they accumulated plenty of savings.

A few months later, the 1917 Ford Model T4 arrived at the main train depot. Ned, asked a long-time friend of his, John Williams, the owner of the only local auto-mechanic repair shop in Greenwood to help him bring his new car home.

John Williams, a successful black businessman, had created many business opportunities for Ned's construction firm particularly when he hired Ned's firm to help in construction of the first movie theatre called the *Dreamland* and a confectionary café in Greenwood neighborhood.

John Williams agreed with Ned's request and drove the car from the train depot to Ned's home while Ned sat on the passenger seat. After handing the car's keys to Ned, he promised that he would teach him how to drive. It did not take Ned long time to learn how to handle his new vehicle.

After returning home from his driving exercise in the nearby open field, he complained to Hannah, "This machine is fun to drive but it behaves like a horse sometimes. It wants to move too fast even when I want it to go slow."

Smiling broadly, Hannah replied, "Try hollering at it and smacking the machine's rear as you always did with our poor horse."

A few weeks later, on a Sunday morning, Ned took Hannah, Joe and Nancy in his new automobile to the church services at Mount Zion Baptist Church on Greenwood Avenue.

On the way back home, Hannah, sitting in the front passenger side, told Ned with a broad grin on her face that she enjoyed the ride.

"You know Ned, I'd prefer our old horse-buggy. This machine too noisy and somehow it ain't smelling so good."

Looking at Hannah lovingly, Ned replied, "You mean that you'd prefer smelling horse's manure? Don't you worry, in time you'll get used to smelling the exhaust fumes as well."

•••

By the end of 1918, with its major business establishments concentrated on the crossroads of Greenwood Avenue and Archer Street, a special commercial block became a prime business location that attracted law offices, drugstores, beauty parlors, newspaper offices, restaurants, fine hotels and jazz joints. Soon after that noticeable commercial expansion, Tulsa's black neighborhood became known as the *Black Wall Street of America*.

In the meantime, Tulsa's white communities north of the railroad seemed to be content with having a highly commercialized but well segregated black community that was established on south of the railroad line. Each and every day, many colored folks left the Greenwood area to work in the white neighborhoods. When they got paid for their work, they deposited their hard-earned salaries into the white-owned banks. With its rising population, now estimated to be over ten thousand colored folks, the highly commercialized Greenwood neighborhood was beaming with many commercial and professional activities conducted by black-owned businesses, who also deposited their earnings and profits in the white-owned banks across the railroad tracks. For the time being, all seemed well because the white folks were happy with the subservient colored folks who lived in their own segregated community and behaved according to the expectations of the white communities' elites.

At that time, due to water shortage in Tulsa, a drinking water storage facility was built on a high ground called *Standpipe Hill*, from which one could clearly view the wide stretch of white communities located at the northern side of the railroad tracks. Similarly, facing the southern horizon on the Standpipe Hill, one could easily notice the prominent buildings of the colored neighborhood of Greenwood, including the Mount Zion Baptist Church, the neighborhood hospital, the middle and high school complex named Booker T. Washington, the Dreamland Movie Theatre and the colossal Greenwood Public Library.

•••

One cold winter morning in 1919, Nancy was not able to wake up. Ned immediately took her to the neighborhood hospital a few blocks away. Doctors informed Ned that Nancy had a stroke during her sleep. The following morning, she died in the hospital. The same afternoon following the church services, she was buried in the colored cemetery of Greenwood.

After the burial ceremony, on their way home Hannah told Ned she now was ready to retire.

"Today," she softly murmured, "I realized that I ain't young no more."

Ned quickly replied, "You are in excellent shape and in good health. I think you want to retire because of Nancy's death."

"No, that ain't exactly true, but her death made me realize our own situation. We're in our seventies.

These days, I ain't feeling so good. I always feel tired. Every day, as I work at the eatery, I lone for a quiet time at home. I ain't enjoying cooking and cleaning anymore. My eatery's doing very good and I think we gonna be able to sell it for good price. I think you gonna also consider selling your construction business and retire."

"No, I'm not planning to sell my business. Our grandson will inherit the construction business. But I fully understand and respect your decision to sell the eatery and retire."

A few months after that discussion, Hannah's eatery was sold to a colored family who recently moved to Greenwood.

Joe Brown had been working happily at his grandfather Ned Blum's construction firm since his return from the military service in 1918. He got himself a small house to live near the construction firm's office. During the fall of 1919, Joe met his future spouse when he was visiting a sick friend at the neighborhood hospital. Maryann, a tall and well-built dark brown beauty, was a professional nurse at the hospital. She recently moved to Tulsa, Oklahoma after completing her nursing education in a medical school in Atlanta, Georgia.

Soon after meeting Maryann at the hospital, Joe asked her out for a dinner date. A few days later, Joe asked Ned to borrow his car for the evening. Watching Joe drive away, Ned excitedly rushed into the house and reported to Hannah that their grandson borrowed the family car to go out for a date.

Hannah, smiling broadly, responded, "I'm so happy to hear that. It's about time. He is so handsome. I always know, one day some special lady gonna latch unto him to start a family."

That is exactly what was happening and Hannah's wish came true soon. Nearly six months later, one spring evening in April of 1920, he surprised his grandparents by declaring that he was now engaged to his longtime girlfriend named Maryann. He told his grandparents Maryann was working as a nurse in the Greenwood's local hospital. The next day, Joe brought Maryann to the house and introduced her to Ned and Hannah.

In October of 1920, they were married in the Mount Zion Baptist Church. The wedding ceremony was attended by many black residents of Greenwood, members of the American Indian community living in the neighborhood and a few white friends of the family from the other side of the railroad tracts.

Immediately after the wedding, Joe and Maryann Brown moved into their own house on the street behind the construction firm. The house was purchased and rebuilt by Ned's company and immaculately furnished with many furniture pieces personally designed by Hannah and handmade by Ned.

On New Year's Eve 1921, the whole family celebrated the new year in Joe and Maryann's new house. During the dinner party, Ned informed Joe that he would soon retire from his construction firm.

"My dear grandson Joe," he gleefully said, "Soon I will turn the business completely over to you. After that, your grandmother and I will enjoy our old age in the tranquility of our home."

With a very happy smile on her face, Hannah added, "But we ain't gonna mind if you and your future children disturb our peace of mind by visiting us frequently."

A month later, Hannah lost the use of her legs due to diabetic complications. She was able to move around the house on a wheelchair that was built by Ned. He moved their bedroom to the first floor and did his best to take good care of Hannah and meet her daily needs.

Every evening after dinner, they took refuge in their reading room with a library full of books. Often, taking a break from intensive reading, they talked about their never-ending adventures in search of a secure and healthy place to live. Starting at a Mississippi cotton plantation and ending in their present house in a dusty black neighborhood of Greenwood in Tulsa, Oklahoma, they talked about many of their adventures until the late hours of the evening.

One late evening, Hannah, closing the book she was reading looked at Ned lovingly and said, "Last year I became home bound by choice and this year because of illness and old age, I became wheelchair bound. I'm sorry Ned from now on I'm gonna be completely dependent on you."

Looking at her affectionately Ned disagreed, "That is not completely true my dear. Even after being bound to a wheelchair, you still are able to prepare delicious dishes for us to enjoy."

Reaching out to the side table full of books, Ned grabbed a pack of playing cards that he recently bought during his shopping trip in Greenwood Avenue.

169

"Last week Joe taught me a card game that I really enjoyed. It is called *Bridge*. Would you like me to teach you?"

"Of course, you may; I ain't able to walk but I still can think."

A few minutes later, realizing the complex nature of the new card game, Hannah commented, "Thanks to God, my mind still in good shape. Otherwise, I ain't able to grasp this complicated card game."

During the next four months all was well in Tulsa and in the black neighborhood of Greenwood. But on May 30th 1921, a young colored man named Dick Rowland, a shoeshine boy working at a major white-owned hotel in Tulsa, caused an incident that ruined everything in Greenwood for good.

As reported by the police, in the hotel's elevator Dick Rowland had made inappropriate advances on a young white woman elevator-operator named Sarah Page. Upon reaching the main floor, Sarah Page started screaming. Before anyone could approach the elevator, Dick Rowland ran away from the hotel to hide in his home in Greenwood. A few hours later he was arrested by Tulsa's police deputies and was placed in the courthouse jail on the corner of Sixth Street and Boulder Avenue near the railroad crossing.

This rather sensitive matter would have worked itself out peacefully if it was allowed to proceed with the usual legal procedures of the police and the court authorities that had included a member of a black law office in Greenwood. Unfortunately, immediately following the incident someone in the police force informed the local white newspaper, *The Tulsa Tribune.* The owner of the newspaper, Richard Jones was a well-known white supremacist and a longtime member of the local chapter of the racist, segregationist organization called Ku Klux Klan. Richard Jones, as the newspaper's chief editor, quickly wrote an editorial piece that was published in that afternoon's edition and immediately circulated in the streets of Tulsa.

In his editorial comment, Richard Jones inappropriately misinformed the public by stating that what had happened that morning at the hotel's elevator was an attempted rape of an underage white woman by a colored man. He finished his editorial note by concluding that the negro rapist, now in police custody, should immediately be lynched.

The next day, early in the morning of 31st of May 1921, the news about the alleged attempted rape had reached almost all the white households of Tulsa as well the colored residents of Greenwood. By mid-morning, hundreds of white men had converged in front of the courthouse where Dick Rowland was being held in jail. As the angry white men in front of the courthouse shouted that they wanted to hang the rapist negro, the police chief William McCullough, realizing the sudden development of an extremely dangerous situation outside, urgently prepared to transfer the prisoner to a more secure facility on the other side of town.

As this was going on in front of the courthouse, hearing about the possibility that a negro named Dick Rowland might be lynched by a white crowd, Joe joined a few of his former colored veteran friends at the Mount Zion Baptist Church's front yard. After several hours of heated discussions, the armed colored veterans decided to inform the police chief that they would not allow a lynching to take place.

On the church lawn, a small group of armed colored veterans was chosen to walk across the railroad to the courthouse to make sure that the angry white mob would not be allowed to enter the courthouse to hang Dick Rowland.

As this small group of veterans with rifles hanging over their shoulders walked in a disciplined military fashion toward the courthouse, a large group of armed black veterans, including Joe, lined shoulder to shoulder near the railroad lines to watch their comrades slowly make their way to the courthouse on the other side of the railroad tracks.

The small group of armed colored veterans was able to walk through the agitated white crowd and reached the courthouse without any incident. The police chief and a few of his deputies came out and stood in front of the main door of the courthouse. The police chief William McCullough told the black veterans not to worry about the possibility of the white mob entering the facility. He assured the safety of Dick Rowland and ordered the black veterans to go back to their neighborhood. The leader of the black veterans named Big Sam, in agreement with the police chief, informed him that they would return to their neighborhood.

"But," he shouted, "if the white mob would attack the courthouse, many armed black men waiting on the other side of the tracks would rush here to protect the life of Dick Rowland."

Responding to Big Sam's words, Chief McCullough again assured the safety of Dick Rowland and ordered the colored veterans to go back to their neighborhood.

As the small group of armed colored veterans with rifles on their shoulders passed again through the agitated but seemingly unarmed white mob, everything seemed going well until one white man pulled out a hidden handgun from his side pocket and started to shoot at the colored veterans walking away in an orderly fashion.

Hearing the gunshot and seeing one of their comrades fell on the ground, well-trained colored veterans, quickly took positions and fired at the white crowd that were preparing to charge toward them. Accurate shootings by the colored veterans resulted in wounding of many whites who quickly scattered away from the well-prepared former colored soldiers. Seeing the white crowd scatter, the black veterans then ran across the railroad tracks toward the safety of their well-armed compatriots waiting at the Standpipe Hill. Expecting that they soon would be attacked by the large white mob, the former black soldiers quickly prepared themselves to defend their community.

As the colored veterans were preparing to defend their community, Joe, tightly holding onto his rifle, ran back to his office that was hardly a block away from the church. At the office, he emptied all his cash from the company safe into a large envelope. On his way home, he remembered that Maryann was on duty at the hospital. He changed direction and walked speedily toward the hospital. At the hospital, he found Maryann at the nurses' station. He handed her the envelope full of cash and told her to go to his grandparents' house after completing her work.

In response, Maryann told Joe that Ned and Hannah were in the hospital early in the morning. When Joe inquired about the reason of their hospital visit, Maryann told him that Hannah was not feeling so well that morning, so they came to meet with her doctor.

Joe reminded Maryann to remain at his grandfather's house until he showed up there. He then rushed back to the Mount Zion Church to join his veteran friends now numbering nearly fifty angry young black men ready to defend Greenwood.

During that afternoon and the rest of the evening hours, many well-armed white men, supported by the Tulsa's police force, prepared to attack the armed colored veterans now joined by hundreds of armed young men of Greenwood neighborhood. This large and well-armed group composed of young black men had congregated around the Standpipe Hill near the Mount Zion Baptist Church. They were now fully ready to stand their ground and defend their community.

Arriving at Joe's grandparents' house, Maryann knocked on the door. When there was no answer, she noticed Ned's car was not there. She could not imagine where they could have gone since their departure from the hospital. She sat on the steps of the front porch to wait for them.

An hour later, Ned, parked his car in front of the house. As he was attempting to get Hannah out of the vehicle to carry her home, Maryann rushed toward him to help.

"What are you doing here, Maryann?" asked Ned worriedly.

"Joe asked me to be with you and Hannah. Haven't you heard the news? Everyone is expecting a bloody battle between the colored and white folks around Standpipe Hill."

"Yes, I've heard something about that while we were in the grocery store. Some people also mentioned to me soon the National Guard troops would be in Tulsa to prevent a bloody conflict. Where is Joe?"

"He joined his veteran friends to protect our neighborhood."

As they carried Hannah home, Ned realized the seriousness of the situation. After placing Hannah on her wheelchair, he asked Maryann to remain in the house.

"Where're you going?" asked Maryann.

"I'll visit my Indian friend Big John's shop. He'll tell me all about what is going on in Tulsa."

Big John welcomed Ned to his shop and told him what he had heard from a few of his white customers.

"Because of the newspaper editorial," he said calmly, "a large white crowd came to the courthouse to lynch the colored boy accused of attempting to rape a young white woman. Apparently, yesterday the shoeshine boy Diamond Dick started this mayhem by chasing after a white girl in the hotel he was working."

"Who exactly told you what had happened?"

"I had a talk with black deputy Barney Cleaver after he came this morning to Miss Damie's boarding house to arrest Diamond Dick. Do you know that boy?"

"I've seen Miss Damie's adopted son around her boarding house. He appears to be a half-witted young man. Do you know why he's called 'Diamond Dick'?"

"After he started to work as a shoeshine boy in that hotel, he bought himself a hefty diamond ring. He wears it when he shines white men's shoes. After what he supposedly did yesterday morning at the hotel, for sure, he is a half-witted stupid boy."

"Exactly what did he do?"

"Deputy Barney told me he fondled a white elevator girl. For that silly attempt he might be lynched."

"Why do you say that?"

"I guess you haven't heard. Yesterday afternoon the Tulsa's white-owned newspaper printed an editorial asking for the colored rapist to be lynched. Hearing about Diamond Dick might get lynched a few colored veterans, armed with rifles, marched this morning to the courthouse and offered the police chief assistance against the white mob gathered in front of the courthouse. After Chief McCullough refused their assistance, the colored veterans decided to go back to

Greenwood. Unfortunately, as they were marching back, a battle between the white mob and the colored veterans took place. As a result of that conflict, five white men and one colored veteran were killed. The white community is now furious and vengeful. I hear that they're now preparing to attack Greenwood."

"I heard at the grocery store this morning that a large regiment of national guards from Oklahoma City were on their way to Tulsa to prevent a bloodbath."

"That may be true, but I am not so sure that they'd get here on time to prevent the angry white men from attacking the black neighborhood."

Now looking very solemn and seriously worried, Ned replied, "This sounds very threatening and dangerous. What do you suggest we do now?"

"I was planning to visit my family at the reservation next week. But I think now may be the good time to go away from Greenwood until all's back to normal. Early tomorrow morning I'll leave town for the reservation."

Staring at Ned with a serious glare, Big John continued, "You and Hannah are welcome to join me. When all the violence has stopped and the dust has settled, we'll come back."

Recalling many of the serious threats they faced during the Wilmington race riots a quarter century earlier, Ned agreed with Big John's proposal.

"It's a good suggestion. I agree we should go away during this threatening conflict. Unfortunately, because of her health condition, Hannah cannot handle such a long trip. I think my grandson Joe and his wife Maryann should join you. Regardless of how the confrontation ends, as a former colored veteran, Joe might get into a serious trouble with the law. I think he and his wife should go with you to the reservation."

As Ned was preparing to leave the shop, Big John asked him if he had any guns to protect his family if whites attack Greenwood.

"Yes, I have a rifle, a revolver and enough ammunition. I hope I don't need to use them. See you early tomorrow morning. I'll make sure Joe and Maryann will be ready to join you."

Ned was back home before dinner time. He quickly prepared the car for the next day's trip to the Chickasaw reservation. Then, he and Maryann prepared a quick dinner. During the subdued, silent dinner, Ned and Maryann did not talk about what was going on in Tulsa. They did not want to disturb Hannah's peace of mind,

It was after midnight, Joe, his shirt soaked in blood, suddenly appeared in Ned's living room. He had a slight bullet wound on his right shoulder. Maryann after checking his shoulder declared that it was just a flesh wound. As Maryann was dressing Joe's wound, Hannah, suddenly waking up, shouted from the bedroom, asking what was going on.

Ned went to the bedroom and told Hannah what had happened. When she heard Joe had been wounded, Hannah started to cry.

Holding her tightly, Ned carried her to her wheelchair. He then pushed the wheelchair into the living room. Fully in shock, Hannah loudly asked Joe, "What happened to you? Why did you get shot?"

As Maryann treated his shoulder wound, Joe told the family about the bloody battle against the white mob that attacked Mount Zion Church.

"We killed many of them white devils but there were so many, so they drove us out of the church grounds. Many of my fellow veteran friends were killed. After I got hit, I hid behind the church and at the first opportunity I ran away here. I don't know what's happening now around Mount Zion Church."

When Joe finished talking, Ned told him and Maryann about Big John's plan to leave Greenwood early in the morning before dawn.

"Joe, I am sure the police will be after you and your surviving veteran friends who fought against the white mob. Big John will stop by our house before dawn to take you both with him to the Chickasaw reservation. I think you should take my car and follow him. You should return here when all is quiet here in Greenwood."

After remaining silent for a moment, Ned continued, "Hannah and I'll stay home. I don't think Hannah can handle such a long road trip. I know you worry about us but our house is not so close to Greenwood Avenue. We might be spared from a mob attack."

Looking intensely at his grandson and Maryann, he continued, "At the Chickasaw reservation, you'll be safe. Now, you should get ready to go. Big John will be here in a couple of hours. He knows the local roads very well. So, you follow him to reach the reservation."

Unhappy with his grandfather's decision to remain in Greenwood, Joe complained, "I don't think we should leave you two here. Please reconsider your decision to remain in this house."

Ned calmly replied, "I've already told you the reason why we're staying behind. Because of Hannah's condition, we cannot travel. Now, don't you worry, we'll be all right."

Ned got up and went to the entry hall to get his car keys. Handing the keys to Joe, he asked, "Are you going to be able to drive with one hand?"

"I think I'll do fine. But if it hurts too much, Maryann could help me change gears."

Soon after Joe and Maryann finished getting ready to travel, they all sat around the dining table and had some coffee and light breakfast Maryann had prepared. They finished eating a few minutes after five o'clock in the morning. Suddenly everyone was jolted by a loud siren emanating from the railroad station. They were not aware that the siren was to announce the start of a major mob attack on Greenwood.

Soon after the siren stopped blaring, Big John's two-horse carriage arrived and parked in front of the house. Big John rushed into the house and announced that the angry white mob will soon cross the railroad tracks to attack Greenwood.

As he was pushing Hannah in her wheelchair to the front porch, Ned quickly asked Big John about the arrival of the National Guard regiment. Big John told him that he had not heard any news about soldiers' arrival.

"If they'd arrive on time," Ned declared, "all the bloodshed and destruction of property might be prevented."

Hannah, pulling on Ned's arm got his attention.

"Ain't you forgetting that in Wilmington and Memphis army troops were around and they chose to let the white mob destroy the colored community? So, there ain't no need raising your hopes for them soldiers come here and save us."

The sun was about to rise, so Big John bid his farewell to Ned and Hannah and said, "May God protect you! I hope I'll see you both soon."

After giving a warm hug to his grandfather, Joe moved toward Hannah in the wheelchair. Getting on his knees, gave his grandmother a big hug and said, "I love you Grandma. May God protect you both!"

As they walked shoulder to shoulder into the front yard, Ned pulled his grandson away from the porch where Hannah was sitting nervously in her wheelchair and watching them. When he was sure that they were far away from Hannah, he stopped and whispered to Joe, "Don't come back to Greenwood. If you do, you'll spend many years in jail. Wait a few days in the reservation and then drive west until you reach the Pacific Ocean. Start a new life somewhere in California. Maryann told me that you have the company cash with you. That was a very smart decision. You'll need that money to start a new life. I'll sell the company and your house as soon as possible and send you the cash. When you arrive at your new destination, let us know as soon as possible"

Before getting into the car, Joe hollered at Big John, "Don't you think you should follow me with your horse buggy all the way to the reservation?"

Smiling, Big John loudly replied, "No, you should follow me. Don't you worry! My buggy with two horses would go as fast as your automobile. Furthermore, you don't really know the way to the reservation. If you take a wrong turn, your vehicle might not survive the bumpy rural dirt roads. You just follow my lead."

Ned, standing next to Hannah on the wheelchair, stood on the porch for a long time watching them ride away from the house. They waved at them until the horse buggy of Big John and the car driven by Joe finally disappeared over the distant southern horizon.

Ned, after pushing the wheelchair back into the house, prepared two cups of coffee and joined Hannah in the living room. As they sipped their morning coffee, they talked about the previous days' affairs.

Appearing uneasy and disturbed about what was going on in Greenwood, Hannah asked, "What you think gonna happen now?"

"I'm sure the National Guardsmen from Oklahoma City already have arrived at Tulsa. The soldiers will make sure there isn't any bloodshed. I remember you told me earlier even if the soldiers arrive on time, they won't do anything to protect our neighborhood. I sincerely hope you're wrong."

Hannah was not wrong at all about what the soldiers would do when they reached Tulsa. The National Guard troops travelling on a train had arrived in Tulsa at four o'clock in the morning, exactly one hour before the loud siren signaling the beginning of the white mob's attack to destroy the colored neighborhood. Ned was wrong in assuming that the National Guardsmen upon arrival in Tulsa would prevent the planned bloody white mob attack on the colored residents of Greenwood. Actually, after arriving in Tulsa's train station and after being briefed by the mayor of Tulsa about the planned attack, the commander of the troops, General Charles Barrett, decided not to interfere with what was about to happen. With such a callous and inappropriate decision, the commanding officer of the National Guards allowed the whole black neighborhood of Greenwood to be completely destroyed and hundreds of its residents be slaughtered.

...

It was still early in the morning when Ned suddenly woke up from his slumber on the couch. Hearing sounds of gunshots coming from streets hardly a few blocks away, Ned speedily got off the couch and shouted at Hannah sleeping on her wheelchair to wake up. He then ran to the kitchen closet where he kept his rifle and a loaded revolver. After loading the rifle, he placed it near the front door and murmured, "I guess the national guard regiment hasn't arrived yet."

He quickly moved a chair next to Hannah and sat down. After getting the revolver cocked, he handed her the gun.

"Be very careful, it's ready to fire. So, keep it under your blanket. When it's absolutely necessary just point the gun and squeeze the trigger. If you need to fire the gun again to protect yourself, you have to cock the gun. Can you do that?"

As Ned showed her how to cock the gun, Hannah complained, "Ned, you know I ain't fired a gun never in my life. I ain't sure I can do it now."

"If this vicious mob reaches our street and our home, we have no choice but to defend ourselves. You have to do this to protect yourself."

After receiving a nod from Hannah, Ned pushed Hannah's wheelchair to the far corner of the living room. He then carried the large leather armchair to the main entry door of the house. After opening the front door, he lifted the armchair and placed it upside down in front of the open front door. He reached for his rifle. Getting it ready to fire at anyone who would dare to approach his house, he prayed to the Lord that their house would be spared from a deadly attack. He then turned toward Hannah and shouted, "Hannah, if we don't survive this, I want you to know that I loved you each and every day of our life we spent together."

Hannah, tears pouring down her wrinkled cheeks, tried to respond to Ned's kind loving words but could not. Finally, she was able to whisper, "I love you too, Ned."

Nearly half an hour later, a group of armed young white men reached a street nearby Ned and

Hannah's house. As the rioters shot at entry doors and windows of the houses nearby, they also threw torches to burn them down.

Ned, hearing the noisy crowd coming closer to his house, got his rifle ready and aimed to shoot. When a small group young white men with rifles in their hands suddenly appeared in front of his house, Ned quickly shot with great accuracy taking two of them down. The others quickly ran away and disappeared from his view.

Ned, while reloading his rifle, turned toward Hannah and shouted, "I got two of them white devils. Others ran away."

As he finished his words, the back door was kicked wide open. Two white men rushed through the kitchen into the living room. Seeing the white man pointing his gun at him, Ned fired his rifle at the same time the intruder fired his.

Hannah first saw the white guy fall backward with the fatal shot from Ned's rifle. Then, turning her head toward Ned, Hannah noticed Ned was lying motionless next to a growing pool of blood in front of the overturned armchair.

Horrified, she remained silent and held the gun in her hand tightly. She suddenly noticed the other intruder standing motionless in the middle of the living room. The intruder then raised his rifle to shoot at Ned who remained still on the bloody floor. Realizing his prey was already dead; he did not squeeze the trigger. As he was slowly turning around to leave the house, he noticed an old black lady sitting in a wheelchair in the far corner of the room. Walking slowly toward the wheelchair, he raised his rifle and aimed to shoot.

Before the armed man could get any closer, Hannah pointed the revolver hidden under the blanket at him as best as she could. She closed her eyes and she squeezed the trigger. The noise and the backward kick of the gun in her hand forced her to open her eyes. She saw the white man's horrified face with wide open eyes staring at her. The wounded man then slowly fell backward on the floor and remained motionless.

After a few minutes of complete silence, another group of armed white men appeared in front of the house and threw several flaming torches into the living room through the open door and the broken windows. Soon after that, the fire quickly spread and engulfed most everything in the living room.

Seeing the curtains and furniture in flames, Hannah closed her eyes and whispered, "I ain't gonna die burning alive." She glanced at Ned's body that was about to be engulfed in flames and murmured, "Ned, my love, I'm gonna be with you soon in the real paradise!"

Feeling the unbearable heat of the flames slowly approaching her. she turned the revolver around pointing it at her heart and placed her right thumb on the trigger. Getting ready to pull the trigger, suddenly her whole life quickly passed through her mind. Her youth as Kangela in her parent's house in a small village in West Africa; her sad seafaring journey on a slave ship where her mother killed herself; arriving in New Orleans and seeing her father for the last time and the hard times she endured as a slave named Hannah on a Mississippi cotton plantation.

A pleasant smile had suddenly appeared on her face when she remembered falling in love with Ned; their adventurous travel to Memphis and moving to Wilmington where years later they lost their only daughter Sarah and son-in law Sam; then their escape to Springfield with their grandson Joe and finally getting on the train to escape from Springfield to have a new life in the colored neighborhood of Tulsa.

With tears running down her sunken cheeks, Hannah pulled the trigger. The gun did not fire. Hannah, with a sad smile on her wrinkled face, realized that she had forgotten to cock the revolver. Feeling the rush of hot flames coming at her, she hurriedly cocked the gun and fired it straight into her heart.

...

On the first day of June 1921, the colored neighborhood of Greenwood in Tulsa, Oklahoma was completely destroyed by the racist white residents of the city. Hundreds of members of the prosperous negro community were killed, their homes and businesses were looted and many buildings were completely destroyed. The thousands of surviving negroes were placed in detention camps in Tulsa. Many of the prominent black-owned properties and public buildings were looted and then burned down. These included the Mount Zion Baptist Church, the neighborhood hospital, the Booker T. Washington High School, Dreamland Movie Theatre and the black-owned Stratford Hotel.

During the coming days, many bloated bodies of colored folks were recovered from the Arkansas River that passed behind the black neighborhood of Greenwood.

As the prosperous black community of Greenwood was completely destroyed and many of its residents were killed, the police force of Tulsa and the recently arrived Oklahoma National Guardsmen just stood by and allowed the whole bloody carnage to take place.

An immediate investigation conducted by the white supremacist State Government of Oklahoma of that time had officially declared that the colored residents of Greenwood, led by a few former negro soldiers, started the whole bloody confrontation with the whites living in Tulsa. So, at the end, such official declaration blamed the entire uprising and its consequences on the colored residents of Greenwood.

•••

About a month later, Joe and Maryann Brown, driving Ned's car, left the Chickasaw reservation for the west coast. After a weeklong drive, they reached the shores of the Pacific Ocean near the city of Los Angeles. They decided to settle in a black neighborhood near the center of the city.

A short time later, Joe found a job in a local carpentry shop making furniture and Maryann also got employed as a nurse at the local hospital. Within a year, with the money he brought from Greenwood, Joe opened his own carpentry workshop.

Soon after settling in Los Angeles, Joe wrote a letter to his grandfather, letting him know he had done exactly what he was asked to do. When he did not receive a reply from his grandfather, he sent a letter to Big John at his shop in Greenwood. He did not receive a reply from Big John as well. As a last resort, he sent a letter to the Chickasaw Reservation Tribal Office, addressing it to Big John.

More than a month later, Joe received a reply from Big John. In his letter Big John informed Joe that his grandparents were killed during the race riots and all of their properties were destroyed. He wrote that his shop was also destroyed during the bloody riot.

Big John ended his latter by stating, "*Because of that horrible, bloody uprising, I moved away from Greenwood. I now live in the reservation.*"

Nearly four years later, Joe and Maryann had a son. They named him Ned, after his great grandfather. Not long after his son's birth, Joe felt he needed a definite closure regarding his grandparents' death. He decided to take a trip to Tulsa, Oklahoma.

After a long Greyhound bus trip, he got off the bus at the downtown bus station in Tulsa. After a short walk, he found his way to the old train station. He continued walking toward Standpipe Hill. Arriving at the old water depo, he turned toward where the

Greenwood neighborhood used to be. From this highpoint, all he saw was a long stretch of horrible landscape full of scattered remnants of burned down, charred buildings. Remembering that during that bloody ominous night he and his veteran friends had fought against the attacking white racists, he could not hold back his tears. He got on his knees and bowed his head to pray for his friends who were killed in that bloody onslaught.

Getting back on his feet, Joe turned around and looked down at the vast white neighborhoods on the other side of the railroad tracts. Noticing many newly built houses on their outskirts, he thought, *"After destroying our neighborhood and murdering many of its residents, including many of my friends and my grandparents, these racist white folks continue to prosper and live their lives as if nothing ever happened. Do they ever remember the prosperous Greenwood community and notice at all the desolation and ruined lives that they had left behind? While I was living here in Greenwood, I was fully aware of the apparent dislikes and prejudices many white folks had toward us colored folks, but I never understood their reasons for such a strong racial hatred that forced them to viciously destroy our community and kill many of its residents. I now realize that following the civil war, the newly liberated former slaves became the victims of highly aggressive and institutionalized members of white supremacy."*

As he turned his back to the white neighborhoods, he murmured, "When will this tragic saga end, if ever?"

He then ventured into remaining tragic landscape of the destroyed Greenwood neighborhood. He walked around to locate his grandparents' house. After a long search, he was able to identify the burned down house where Ned and Hannah had perished. He prayed for the souls of his beloved grandparents and also for his parents who were killed during the 1898 Wilmington, North Carolina race riots.

He then walked back to the city center to catch the bus back to Los Angeles. As he waited in front of the greyhound bus station, Joe noticed a middle age black man sweeping the front of a liquor store across the street. He approached the man and asked if he was from the old Greenwood neighborhood.

The man stopped his sweeping and nervously stared at Joe.

"I came here to Tulsa from Austin, Texas two years ago. I ain't heard much about the destroyed black neighborhood. White folks ain't talking about that place no more."

"So, you're saying there are no survivors that you know of from the old Greenwood community?"

As he resumed sweeping the storefront, he responded, "Yes sir, that is exactly what I'm saying. There ain't no one from that old destroyed neighborhood remain here in Tulsa. They all gone. Why are you so curious about that old ruined negro neighborhood?"

"I grew up in that neighborhood and I was there when it was attacked and destroyed by the white racists six years ago."

"I see what you mean! But I ain't getting it; why you come back?"

"I came back for closure and for the memory of my grandparents, who were killed here. I thank you for talking to me."

With a sorrowful face, the man sullenly replied, "You're welcome. Sorry about your grandparents. You make sure you have safe trip back home."

...

Similar to Wilmington's bloody riots of 1898, Tulsa riot of 1921 also became a forgotten incident under a well-sustained, long-lasting cover up efforts by the Federal authorities and the State of Oklahoma. Such cover up efforts were followed by a long-lasting conspiracy of silence that kept this bloody affair away from a possible Federal Government scrutiny or any substantive national press coverage for almost a century.

In Tulsa, following the vicious race riots, no one was ever prosecuted for the bloody killings and none of the black residents of Greenwood were ever compensated for their losses. After that racist uprising in 1921 and during the coming several decades, the city of Tulsa, for that matter the whole State of Oklahoma, was controlled by a white supremacist, KKK-affiliated political power structure.

In June of 1921, a loud scream of a young white female that had suddenly emanated from an elevator of a white-owned hotel in Tulsa, Oklahoma, fortunately did not result in the lynching of the young negro man named Dick Rowland. During the bloody uprising, the police had moved him away from the courthouse jail on time.

A few months after the riots, Sarah Page, the screaming young lady, disappeared from Tulsa. Soon after her disappearance, Dick Rowland was released from police custody. The rumor has it that they got together and settled somewhere in the eastern part of the country. One could easily imagine the first conversation these two miscreants had when they got together.

"Why did you scream in the elevator, Sarah?"

"I was really mad at you for what you've said to me the night before."

It seems that a lovers' quarrel may have resulted in the complete destruction the black Greenwood community and killing hundreds of its residents. How sad that it was allowed to happen. However, given the high level of racial hatred that boiled in the hearts of the white supremacist citizens of Tulsa, all they needed was an excuse to destroy a thriving black community.

What happened in the Greenwood neighborhood of Tulsa, Oklahoma was the beginning of the end of the racist, irrational political doctrine called 'Separate but Equal', which falsely assumed that such a political strategy could create separate living spaces under the equal opportunity principle for the emancipated former slaves. However, since the end of the civil war in 1865, the formation of racist settlement policies that were based on such segregationist political thought soon turned into highly inflammable political tinderboxes that generated many bloody race riots invariably initiated by the supremacist, racist whites in many parts of the United States. Disregarding the numerous race riots that had occurred in various parts of the country and also the pain, destruction and deaths such riots inflicted upon the generations of colored folks, such a racist, segregationist political dogma was unfortunately permitted to exist since the beginnings of the post-civil war era and was allowed to spread all over the country during the coming one hundred years. This in part was due to the loopholes that had existed in the United States' constitutional framework which allowed the systematic misuse of the Federal legal system to embolden the racist, supremacist components of the white power structure in the United States for nearly a century.

August 11, 1965: Watts Neighborhood, Los Angeles

When the Watts race riots suddenly erupted in Los Angeles in August of 1965, it was a very unlucky day for Hannah and Ned's great grandson, also named Ned. He was born in Los Angeles in 1925 and similar to his First World War veteran father Joe, he joined the military during the Second World War and served in the European front to fight against the German forces. He was wounded in the battlefield and sent home only with a military handshake. Unfortunately, during that time, black veterans were not considered for war medals even if they would have deserved one by a distinguished service on the battlefield.

After returning home from the Second World War, Ned Brown had hard time finding any gainful employment. He lived with his mother Maryann and was employed in various part time jobs for several years. Finally, in 1959 he became a full-time federal employee by joining the postal service as a mailman.

As he was delivering mail on that ominous day on August 11, 1965, Ned unexpectedly fell into the cross fire between the police and the black rioters. He was mortally hit by a bullet and died on the pedestrian walkway.

During that particular morning, Ned's mother Maryann, who had retired from her nursing job at a local hospital a year earlier, was called back to duty at the hospital due to the presence of vast numbers of wounded in the emergency room. As she was helping wounded patients, she was approached by a California state trooper. The officer calmly informed her that her son Ned was found dead on a pedestrian walkway lying next to his mailbag.

"Unfortunately," the officer claimed, "your son was in the wrong place at the wrong time. He was accidentally shot during a sudden flare of gunfire between the police and the rioters. You can claim your son's body from the local mortuary."

Standing silently in the middle of a treatment room full of wounded people and hospital personnel, Maryann held back her tears. After the departure of the state trooper, she ran to the nearest restroom, covering her face with her hands, she cried loudly for a long time.

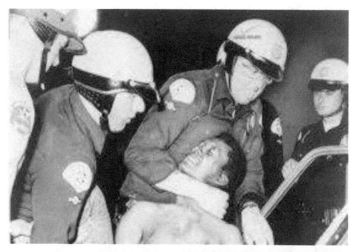

After the end of the race riots a week later, Maryann Brown was able to claim her son's body from the local mortuary. When the responsible person at the mortuary had asked Maryann for a funeral-home address, she told her that the Veteran's Administration would handle the burial. A year earlier, the Veterans Administration made the necessary arrangement for Joe's burial in a veterans' cemetery after he had passed away from a sudden heath attack. She immediately went to the local Veterans Administration building and requested assistance with her son Ned's burial.

For the rest of her remaining days, Maryann had a very lonely life, barely surviving alone in a rundown public housing facility in the miserably poor Watts black neighborhood of Los Angeles. However, until her dying day, she never failed to visit her beloved husband Joe and son Ned every month at the local veterans' cemetery.

Federal Civil Rights Legislation of 1965

Since the end of the civil war in 1865, the civil and political rights of the emancipated former slaves were mostly ignored by the State authorities and Federal Government for nearly a century. In 1965, by passing the federal civil rights legislation in the United

States Congress, the American Government finally took the necessary steps to recognize the undeniable basic civil rights of the colored citizens of the United States.

During the upcoming decade, from 1965 to 1975, many important Federal civil and voting rights legislations were passed by the United States Congress and became the law of the land. However, such necessary and timely establishment of civil and political rights unexpectedly moved the sensitive race relations in America into a new set of untested parameters of racism, which have been clearly exemplified by the rising number of violent interracial conflicts during the second half of the 20th and the first 20 years of the 21st century. There are now ample reasons to acknowledge the uneasy and unsettled race relations in the United States. Now is the proper time to take the necessary policy actions to establish much needed peaceful coexistence of different ethnic and racial entities through a system of equal opportunities based socio-economic integration while preventing the inevitability of destructive evils brought by ethnic and racial conflicts.

Passing federal laws is one thing and implementing the enacted laws fairly and equitably throughout the crusty old racist institutional structures still prevailing in many of the states is another. After initiating necessary efforts to eliminate racially and ethnically biased rules and regulations that still exist in the institutional structures of many states, the struggle to establish a fully integrated, politically balanced socio-economic system with equal opportunities for all might possibly come into existence. If and when such state-wide institutional corrections for racial and ethnic integration could be initiated and activated in each and every state of the Federal Union, then the United States of America, the richest and most technologically developed country in the world, may become a true paradise for all of her citizens regardless of their race and ethnicity.

BIBLIOGRAPHY

Cecelski, David S. and Timothy B. Tyson (1998), *Democracy Betrayed: The Wilmington Race Riots and its Legacy*, Chapel Hill: University of North Carolina Press.

Douglas, Chester (2020), *The Wilmington Insurrection of 1898 (The Democrats, The Secret Nine, and The Rise of White Supremacy)*, Independently Published.

Edmonds, Helen G. (1951), *The Negro and Fusion Politics in North Carolina, 1894-1901*, Chapel Hill: University of North Carolina Press.

Graglia, Richard E. (2017), *Our Plantation: Life on a Southern Cotton Plantation During the Civil War*, Independently Published.

Gordon-Reed, Annette (2021), *On Juneteenth*, Liveright.

Harris, John (2020), *The Last Slave Ships: New York and The End of the Middle Passage*, Yale University Press.

Lowry, Irving E. (2017), *Life on Old Plantation in Ante Bellum Days,* Gyan Books.

Madigan, Tim (2013), *The Burning: The Tulsa Race Massacre of 1921*, Thomas Dunne Books.

Masur, Kate (2021), *Until Justice Be Done: America' First Civil Rights Movement from the Revolution to Reconstruction*, W. W. Horton.

McCoy, David B. (2020), *The 1898 Wilmington North Carolina Coup D'état*, Spare Change Press.

McWhirter, Cameron (2011), *Red Summer: The Summer of 1919 and the Awakening of Black America*, Henry Holt and Co.

Payne, David (2018), *Tulsa's Black Wall Street (A story of Greenwood Oklahoma)*, Independently Published.

River, Charles (2020), *The Tulsa Massacre of 1921*, Independently Published.

Roche, Emma Langton (2021), *The Last Voyage of the Clotilda*, Lulu.com.

World Changing History (2020), *Tulsa Race Massacre of 1921 (*The History of Black Wall Street, and Its Destruction in America's Worst and Most Controversial Racial Riot), Independently Published.

Zucchino, David (2020), *Wilmington's Lie: The Murderous Coup of 1898 and the Rise of White Supremacy,* Atlantic Monthly Press.

BOOKS BY OMER ERTUR
[on amazon.com]

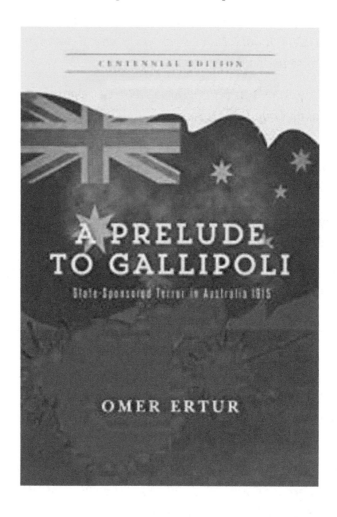